"Jealous, are you?" Colin asked coldly

"Not on your life," Anna snapped.

"What do you care who I spend time with then? If you're so tired of being my fiancée, what difference does it make to you?"

"None," Anna said quickly, trying to open a file drawer.

"I don't believe you," Colin said, striding over and gripping her by the arms, turning her to face him. "What's the matter? Afraid that Cindy Tate might be getting a little of what you want?"

"Of course not!" She twisted to get away from him.

"I'll bet you are," he said, his dark eyes glittering. "I'll say one thing for Cindy Tate, though. At least she doesn't promise more than she delivers!"

Dare To Trust

Anne McAllister

Harlequin Books

TORONTO • NEW YORK • LONDON
AMSTERDAM • PARIS • SYDNEY • HAMBURG
STOCKHOLM • ATHENS • TOKYO • MILAN

Original hardcover edition published in 1985
by Mills & Boon Limited

ISBN 0-373-02721-4

Harlequin Romance first edition October 1985

CHAPTER ONE

'AIN'T he a hunk, honey?' the waitress said to Anna as she banged the cash register drawer shut, her eyes never leaving the lithe young man going out the door.

Ain't he just, Anna Douglas thought, her eyes trailing him unwillingly as he left the tiny road-side restaurant, got into his red Porsche and drove away. 'Sure is,' she said because the waitress was obviously waiting for a confirmation of her description and, as 'hunks' went, he wasn't bad. Being a 'hunk' though, as far as Anna was concerned was not a huge recommendation. Toby after all had been a 'hunk', and look what a rat he had been.

She wondered idly what the waitress would think of Richard Howell, the fiancé she had left back in California. Her ex-roommate, Teri Gibbs, thought Rich was everything a woman could want. He was, too. Dependable, secure, responsible, attractive in his own way, but definitely not a 'hunk'. But that, as far as Anna was concerned, ranked high on the list of things that recommended him. He was everything that Toby was not.

'Just passing through?' the waitress asked, slapping a bowl of chilli and a salad in front of her.

'No. I'm staying. I'll be teaching here starting in the autumn.'

The waitress whistled as she glanced out the dirty window at Anna's beat-up VW with the out-of-state plates. 'Long way from California to Wisconsin. Got a place to stay?'

'With Professor Fielding's family. Do you know them?'

She wasn't surprised when the waitress said that she did. A few minutes' conversation had convinced her that not much happened in this south-western Wisconsin town that the woman didn't know about. 'I thought Mac went to Turkey,' the waitress said.

'Greece,' Anna said. 'On sabbatical for an archae-ological dig. But his son, William, is coming back from Guatemala to teach for him. So I'll be living with him and his sister, Jenny.'

The waitress nodded. 'Nice kid. Bit flighty, but then teenagers often are. More chilli? You're a skinny thing.' She eyed Anna's slender, five-foot-six-inch frame with something akin to pity. 'Ain't seen Will lately. When'd he get back?'

Anna felt a twinge of apprehension. 'This week, I think,' she said with more confidence than she felt. She had gone to his house first and no one was there. That was why she was eating chilli here, killing time before she went back and, she hoped, found someone at home. 'No thanks,' she said as the waitress hovered over her bowl with another helping of chilli. 'Just a bath and bed would do me now.'

She had been on the road since seven that morning, the last leg of her six-day jaunt across the country. All she wanted was to wash the miles off her weary body and collapse. She paid the bill and trudged out to the car, about to get in when she spied a 'phone booth at the filling station across the street. Marvellous. She could call Rich from here and let him know she had arrived. Then, if Fielding weren't home, God forbid, she wouldn't have to tell him so. He was certain she was crazy to have come so far away to take this job and she didn't need anything to go awry and confirm his view.

He answered the 'phone on the third ring as usual.

'It's me! I'm here!' Anna blurted, her apprehensions fading at the sound of his predictably calm voice.

'Where? Fielding's?'

'No, but in Belle River,' she hedged. 'I drove past the house on the way in. It's gorgeous, Rich! Late Victorian brick with huge wraparound porches, lots of chimneys, a tower with a conical roof ...' Her enthusiasm bubbled until she recalled that Rich was a chrome-and-glass, Scandinavian-modern man himself. Then she caught herself up short. 'But no one was home so I ate in a restaurant.'

'I thought they were expecting you.'

'I didn't say what time I was arriving. Just sometime late this week. I mean, if you drive all the way from California to Wisconsin, you don't know the exact hour you'll get in town.'

'I would,' Rich said, which was true. Rich was as predictable as the tide. He lived by timetables and schedules, and Anna lived by intuition, which was why he was in LA at the moment and she was two thirds of the way across the country even though they'd only been engaged five weeks.

'I expect they'll be home soon,' Anna said, writing 'I hope' in the dust on the window of the booth.

'And if they're not?' A sensible question. Part of Rich's attraction was his ability to look at things realistically. But it wasn't helping now when she didn't need realism as much as bolstering.

'They will be,' she said. 'They're expecting me. Anyway, Professor Fielding sent me a key.'

Rich sighed, one of his long-suffering ones that let Anna know he was humouring her. 'All right,' he said, but he didn't sound convinced. Not much she had done since their engagement had convinced Rich of anything except perhaps that she didn't know her own mind. He had found it irrational, to say the least, that she had accepted his proposal on the first of May and had taken a job teaching sixth grade in Belle River, Wisconsin two weeks later. Rich never did anything without plenty of forethought and planning. And it was just such planning that was at least partly why he asked her to marry him. He was thirty-five years old, successful at his job and he'd decided it was time to marry.

It was a wonder, Anna knew, that her actions hadn't prompted him to ask for his ring back. Instead he had just asked, 'Why?' in calm, reasonable tones that made her feel guilty as she mumbled something about 'breathing space' and 'being sure' and 'needing to stand on her own two feet.' She wondered what she'd have done if he had got angry or pleaded with her not to go. But he hadn't. He had considered things for two weeks from every conceivable angle and had finally shrugged and said, 'Okay, I can live with that. Take a year if you need to. It's the sensible thing to do.'

Anna smiled now as she remembered. It hadn't been sensible at all. It had been a knee-jerk reaction to finding herself engaged, a reaction since overlaid with several layers of rationalised common sense. What she needed, she told herself, was to prove that absence really did make the heart grow fonder, that the safe, steady dependable love she felt for Rich would still light up her life even though she was 2,000 miles away. And she needed to know that she wasn't using him, marrying him because she liked him because he wasn't Toby, and because, now that she had lost her first teaching job due to budget cuts, she wasn't saying yes to gain the security he offered. She could prove all that here in Belle River. All she needed was a modicum of independence, a job of her own, a few obstacles to overcome and she would be satisfied. In a year she could go home and never wonder again if the only reason she married Rich was because she couldn't think of a reason why not.

'I'll call you again in a few days,' she told him. 'Once I'm settled.'

'Don't get too settled,' he said, and she could picture the grin on his tanned face. 'Remember, it's only for a year. And beware of single archaeologists, especially ones attracted to auburn-haired, green-eyed beauties like you!'

She wasn't a beauty in the conventional sense, but her fine-boned features, full lips and striking colouring made her attractive to many males. She doubted William Fielding would be one of them. 'Rich! He's engaged!'

'So are you,' he said darkly. 'Just remember to whom!'

'Don't worry,' Anna promised. 'Everything will be fine.'

Rich needn't fret, she thought as she drove back to Fielding's. She knew a good man when she saw one. Even if Will Fielding were as gorgeous as Toby, she had no doubt she could resist the temptation. It might even be easier if he were. Looks after all were no reflection of the inner man. She smiled, feeling more optimistic now that she had the chilli and salad inside her. Maybe Will wouldn't even be there yet. Maybe he would be out with a gorgeous fiancée. In the meantime she would let herself in with the key his father sent her and make herself at home.

There were still no lights on when she drove up in front of the house and dragged her two most essential suitcases on to the front porch. She banged loudly on the front door, but all she heard was a lawn mower down the street and a motorcycle revving its engine in the gravel alley. No sound at all came from within. So this is how Goldilocks felt, Anna thought as she turned the key and pushed open the heavy oak door.

'Anybody home?' she called. Her sandals clicked on the parquet floor of the cavernous entry hall, but she only got an echo for an answer. The blue carpeted front parlour was dim in the evening half light, but she made out a roomful of oak furniture, early 20th century period pieces with a contemporary sofa and chairs that lent a homey atmosphere. It was not the House-and-Garden modern Rich preferred, but she could have spent hours curled in the window seat with a book, enjoying a fire in the marble fireplace and listening to something romantic on the thoroughly modern stereo system in the glass-fronted bookcase on the far wall. She tiptoed through the parlour, attracted by the abundance of books, prints and archaeological artefacts, but feeling increasingly uneasy as every moment passed.

It wasn't just that no one was home. She could have understood that. But everything was so neat, so spotless, so closed up, as if not only Malcolm Fielding had departed for Greece but that Will and Jenny had gone too.

God, I hope not, she thought. What would she do then? She had come in June because Malcolm Fielding had offered her a job typing and doing research for Will who was doing a book on Mayan artefacts. If Will

wasn't here, she would be without a job and, most
likely, without a place to stay too. Well, you wanted
some independence, she reminded herself. But by
independence she wasn't sure she meant jobless and
2,000 miles from home.

A tour through the dining room and den lent further
support to her fears. A thin layer of dust coated
everything and the three-week-old TV guide lay on a
table. But when she opened the door to the blue and
white kitchen she breathed a sigh of relief. Surely no
one would go off to Greece and leave a sinkful of dirty
dishes, half a loaf of bread and a jar of instant coffee
open on the counter. Anna sagged against the
butcherblock table in relief. They must only have left
for the day. She could write them a note and leave it on
the table before she went to bed so they wouldn't
stumble on her unawares.

She hummed now as she went back to the foyer and
picked up her luggage. Grabbing a suitcase in each
hand she began to climb the wide oak stairway, glad
that her optimism was justified and that Rich's
apprehensions had, for once, come to naught. Being
Goldilocks wasn't so bad after all.

'Who the hell are you?'

Anna froze at the sound of a hoarse voice coming
from the top of the stairs. Staring upward she saw a
tall, menacing figure of a man looming in the shadows
of the upstairs hall. One of the three bears? she
wondered. Papa, by the look of him. All fierce and
arrogant.

This was William Fielding? Lord, she hoped not. But
if he wasn't, who was he? And that wasn't an
encouraging line of thought either.

'Who—who are you?' Her voice was a mere croak
and she banged her head on the Boston fern hanging in
the landing window.

'Come up here,' he commanded, ignoring her
question.

Anna didn't move.

'I said, "Come here." ' His voice wasn't so harsh the

second time. Maybe he realised he was scaring her to death.

Reluctantly Anna mounted the stairs, her eyes never leaving him. I could hit him with a suitcase and run, she thought. I could throw it at him and run. I could ... I could ... She knew she could do no such thing.

The man never stopped watching her either. As she got closer she could see that he was fairly tall, certainly dark and undeniably scruffy. A bear wasn't a bad analogy. His hard face wore an expression of arrogant belligerence which was enhanced by the fact that he had neither shaved nor combed his hair for what looked like several days. He wore only a pair of grey track shorts which showed off a lean, well-muscled physique and a tan even darker than her own. She wondered if the waitress would think he was a 'hunk'. Probably. But with that expression he was a hulk more likely, or would be if he gained twenty or thirty pounds. If he was William Fielding she had clearly got more than she had bargained for.

'Now,' he said again as she stood at a disadvantage two steps below him on eye level with his thickly matted chest, 'who are you and what are you doing here?' His voice was low, not thundering at all, but so cold it made Anna shiver.

'I'm Anna Douglas.' She tipped her head back to look into the almost black eyes probing her own. 'And,' she added with every bit of courage she could muster, 'I'm moving in.' It was a gamble certainly, not cowering and apologising which he seemed to expect. But, as her minister father had often said, 'Our Annie doesn't lack spunk,' and if ever spunk seemed called for, now was the time.

'Moving in like hell.' He stared at her, astonished.

'This is Professor Fielding's house?' she pressed him, using his astonishment to her advantage by moving up one step so that he edged backwards.

'Yes.'

'Then I'm moving in. Surely your father mentioned

it,' she went on. What kind of father hired someone to be his son's assistant and failed to tell his son?

The man looked at her almost glazed, as though he didn't follow what she was saying. 'My father?' he echoed dully.

'He said you wanted an assistant. Research, typing, that sort of thing.' He needed a good interpreter more, she thought. He looked as if plain English were beyond him.

'You're her?' A spark of recognition. 'Oh God.'

If there was comfort in that response, it was hard to find. The man rubbed a hand across his face and shook his head as though trying to clear it. Then he stepped back and leaned against the wall, regarding Anna as if she were some lower form of life. 'You didn't get the letter,' he said.

Anna felt an awful sinking feeling grow where her stomach used to be. 'What letter?'

'Not to come. Change of plans. Stay home. No job. That letter.' He sagged slightly and Anna stepped into the hallway, noticing as she did so that he looked very white around the mouth.

'I never got any letter. When did you sent it?'

He shrugged. 'Three, maybe four days ago. I've lost track of time.'

'I left California a week ago,' she told him irritably. After six days on the road she did not need this.

'Hell.'

'My sentiments exactly,' Anna retorted. 'Now what, Mr Fielding?'

'I don't know. You can't stay here.' He straightened up. 'And I'm not Mr Fielding.'

'What do you mean I can't stay here?' Anna demanded. He didn't look fierce at all now, just exhausted. She could see perspiration dotting his forehead beneath spikes of dark brown hair. 'I was offered a job as assistant to William Fielding. How can you tell me I don't have that job? Especially if you're not Will Fielding! Who the hell are *you* anyway?'

He rubbed a weary hand against the back of his neck and shut his eyes briefly as if he wished she'd vanish when he opened them again. 'All right, so you didn't get my letter. I'm sorry.' He didn't look sorry, only annoyed. 'Will's in Guatemala so there isn't any job. Surely you can see that. I came to take his place for the summer. My name is Colin Davies. I'm his cousin.'

So much for trusting one's expectations, Anna thought, her visions of a pleasant summer spent in the company of an affable Will Fielding completely flattened by the presence of a very irritable, virile Colin Davies. It was rather like anticipating a house cat and opening the door to a tiger. Perhaps it was because he looked so undomesticated. Now that she could see him up close she was inclined to agree with what she imagined would be the waitress's estimation of him. Beneath the spiky hair and whiskered face he was more than handsome, however rugged and wild. He only needed to get a haircut, shave, and gain a few pounds and he would be devastating. That and lose the dreadful pallor becoming increasingly apparent on his face. Then he would be a hunk indeed. Anna took a quick step backward.

'I don't understand,' she said. 'Why are you here?'

'Getting well, I hope.' He didn't look optimistic. 'I've got malaria and a spot of some jungle fever. I've had it before. It takes some bed rest and then I'm fine, so . . .' He shrugged. 'Will and I agreed that it made more sense for me to come back and for him to stay and work. I can still teach.'

'But my job . . .'

Colin gave her a pained look, as if she were a particularly pesky child. 'As soon as I get well, I promise I'll leave. Then Will can come home and you can have your damned job. Okay? But in the meantime, you go.'

'No.'

'What?' He looked incredulous.

'I said,"no". Why can't I help you? If you're an archaeologist too you must need . . .'

'I don't need anything. Least of all some female hovering over me.'

'But——'

'No.' It was flat, final. No appeal. 'I always manage fine on my own.' He gave her a grim, tight-lipped smile and put his hand against the wall to steady himself. Anna saw his jaw tighten as if he were making a conscious effort to remain upright. Whatever tropical fever he had, it must be the cause of the pallor, unsteadiness and the glassy, fever-brightness of his eyes.

'I——'

'Go home,' he said roughly.

The fever caused irrationality as well obviously. 'All the way to California?' she mocked. He wasn't going to last much longer without toppling, she could tell.

Colin shrugged. 'As far as you like. There're hotels in town. If you need money I'll give you some. But you can't stay here.' He turned as if he were going to go down the hall to his room to fetch his wallet.

'*Why* can't I stay here?' She was getting angrier by the minute with his high-handed attitude.

'I hate people hovering. I sent Jenny to stay with friends. I just want to be left alone. Hang on, I'll be right back.'

'I don't want your money!' Anna grabbed his arm, but he shook her off and stumbled heavily against the newel post.

'Damn,' he muttered. 'Go back downstairs. I'll bring you a cheque. It's the least I can do.' He took a shaky breath and licked parched lips.

'Don't be so damned stupid! Stop worrying about me and go lie down before you fall down. You look dreadful.' Anna scowled at him. He was visibly trembling now, and she saw him clench his fist to stop his fingers shaking.

'See? Hovering. If you don't want the money, okay. Just go away and leave me alone.' He was hanging on to the newel post, and Anna thought he was going to go green right before her eyes.

His eyes shut briefly and he swayed forward, then mustering strength from somewhere, he turned and bolted down the hall. Dumbstruck, for a moment Anna didn't follow. Then, concerned in spite of what she knew his attitude would be, she followed the sounds of Colin retching to the open doorway of the bathroom. His shoulders were still heaving as he struggled to steady his breathing and Anna noticed the fine sheen of perspiration on his darkly tanned back. He tried to pull himself to his feet but he couldn't stop trembling and, after a moment, sank back on to his knees again.

'Here,' Anna said, going to him instinctively, 'I'll help you.' She had her arm around his back and had lifted one of his over her shoulders before he could protest. Weakly he stumbled to his feet, most of his weight depending on Anna for support.

'It's all right. I can——'

'You can go flat on your nose if I let you,' Anna said with asperity. 'Come on.' She manoeuvred him around in the small bathroom, increasingly dismayed by his feverishness. The feel of his hot, shaking body against hers proved how much sicker he really was than she had first imagined. She didn't dare leave him alone here now even if he wanted her to. 'Which room is yours?'

'You can't . . . I've got to . . .' he protested, making a faint attempt to turn back towards the bathroom which he obviously intended to clean up.

'Never mind,' she said forcefully. He was shaking and she was going to drop him if she didn't get him to his room soon. 'I'll do it. Which room?'

Helplessly he gestured with his head. 'That one.'

It was halfway down the hall on the left and looked more like a second-hand-bookstore-cum-museum than a bedroom. Piles of notebooks and books, bits of pots and heaps of papers were littered across the dresser, desk and bed. Only the last, large and unmade, with tangled sheets and strewn notecards, gave evidence that he actually slept there. He could have fought demons there too from the look of it.

'Wow,' she muttered involuntarily.

'Wow?' Colin's brow lifted in curiosity as Anna lowered him into the armchair by the window.

'Just admiring your dedication.' She waved an arm at the book-covered bed. 'Do you work until you throw up, then start in again?'

'Something like that.' The barest hint of a smile flickered across his harsh face.

'Rest there a moment and I'll straighten it for you.'

The smile vanished. 'No. I'll manage,' he said curtly.

Anna gave him an annoyed look. 'You don't have to prove how tough you are to me. I'll go and clean up the bathroom then.'

Colin eyed her narrowly, looking like he would like to say something scathing if only he could manage it. But the effort must have been too much for he shrugged almost imperceptibly and turned away to glare out the window into the deepening dusk.

My Lord, what have I got myself into now? Anna wondered, thinking for the first time that Rich might possibly be right. But after she had taken care of things in the bathroom, she went across the hall from Colin's room to where she had determined 'her' bedroom to be and flicked on the light. Immediately she saw another reason to dig in her heels. Never in her life had she had such a lovely room as this. With cheerful yellow walls, a marble fireplace, wicker rocker and brass bed complete with a faded, but cheery, patchwork quilt, it fairly shouted a welcome at her.

She ran her hand along the polished brass beadstead and firmly decided that she'd put up with Attila the Hun for this. She might have to, too, she thought wryly, or his present day incarnation anyway. She dragged her suitcases into the bedroom and decided that a change of clothes would do her wonders before another set-to with Colin. Tossing her travelling clothes into the rocker to deal with later, she dressed quickly in a pair of snug faded jeans and a bright yellow T-shirt with a beer advertisement on it. It might not be fancy, but at least it had the virtue of being clean. She tugged a brush through her shoulder length auburn hair, thinking as she considered her weary, wide-eyed face in the mirror above the fireplace that it wasn't a vast improvement.

But it was enough, at least, to give her the courage to go another round with Colin Davies.

Steeled for a confrontation and, surprisingly, looking forward to it, she re-entered his room to find him still sprawled in the armchair, eyes closed, head thrown back. He looked neither fierce nor formidable now, but oddly vulnerable. She could see more clearly the ravages of his illness, the sunken cheeks and sallow complexion, his bony ribs and hips that made her feel strangely maternal and full of longings to comfort him and fatten him up.

Hovering, she reminded herself sharply. I must be out of my mind. He has no use for me whatsoever, and if I've any doubt, I've only got to ask him. She didn't need to for at that moment he opened his eyes and all his earlier hostility returned in an instant.

'How do you feel?' she asked, trying to ignore the tension between them as she stood in the doorway staring at him.

'Better. Sorry about that.' His voice was expressionless, as if what had happened had happened to someone else.

'No problem.' She moved to the end of his bed and began to remove the books so she could straighten the bed and change the sheets. 'Where are the clean sheets?'

'Never mind. It's all right.'

Anna rolled her eyes. The sheets were grey and dingy. 'Humour me. I adore changing sheets.' She gave him a saccharine smile.

Colin looked murderous. 'Down the hall on the left,' he growled finally, when staring her down failed. Then he closed his eyes dismissing her. But when she returned he opened them and watched her, hawklike and suspicious, and the moment her hand touched one of his papers he snapped, 'Leave those alone!'

'Do you intend to sleep with them?'

'I'll manage.'

'Famous last words,' she mocked gently and a faint red crept into his cheeks. But sensing that it really mattered, she went on, 'If you'll tell me what order to put them in, I'll stack them by the wall.'

He stared at her a long moment as though debating whether to trust her, then drew a long breath and grudged, 'Okay.'

She moved the papers carefully, complying exactly with his directions, intrigued by the cryptic notes on them, impressed by the firm, black handwriting and the meticulous neatness which belied the rats-nest chaos in which she found them on his bed. Obviously he was a careful, responsible scholar even if he was a bear. Some of his abruptness abated as she followed his instructions to the letter, but when she finished and offered him a hand to pull himself up, the barrier between them clanked down again.

'I can manage by myself, Miss Douglas,' he said stiffly, ignoring her outstretched hand and staggering to his feet unaided.

Stubborn devil, she thought, reminded of the wounded cat she had once patched up only to have it turn around and bite her. But she withdrew her hand, stepping back, and contented herself with saying, 'You can reject my help, but I think you should call me Anna. It's hard to be formal with the person who's just mopped up after you.' It was not a nice thing to say, but Colin Davies was not being a particularly nice person.

'You didn't have to,' he barked. He took the few steps from the chair to his bed carefully and dropped into it with the relief of a camel drive come to an oasis. Settling against the pillows he sighed heartily, then looked at Anna with a sort of wary sheepishness. 'Sorry,' he muttered. 'And thanks.'

It wasn't much, but from what she'd seen of Colin so far, it was all she was likely to get. And more than she'd ever got from that rotten cat. 'You're welcome.' She drew the top sheet over him. 'If you need me, call.'

'I'll——'

'Manage,' she finished with more than a hint of exasperation. 'Yes, you probably will. But in any case,

I'll be right across the hall. Good night.' She didn't wait for a reply. She didn't think she'd want to hear it.

Stupid, perverse pig. Living with him wasn't going to be any picnic, she thought as she went back into her room and flopped across the firm, wide bed. Accustomed to the calm, steadying presence of Rich Howell, she felt as if she had just gone ten rounds with a grizzly bear.

'Stubborn idiot,' she mumbled. 'Mr Independence Personified!'

She wanted to thump him. How dare he tell her to find a hotel? Did he think she was going to compromise his virtue? There was a laugh. Colin Davies looked nothing if not experienced, however independent he was. The more she saw of him, the more she was sure the waitress would have been charmed. He had a presence, a magnetism she would have adored. Anna wrinkled her nose in distaste. He was definitely the sort of man who found a use for women in his life even if it wasn't for hovering. Or caring.

Just like Toby.

Damn, yes, he even resembled Toby—the dark hair and stubborn jaw, the panther-like eyes. She thumped her pillow irritably, angry again at the thought of Toby's practiced charm, his blatant sex appeal, and his complete lack of commitment. Was Colin Davies the same sort of man? Very likely, she thought, remembering his harsh words and hard eyes. Just the sort of man to steer clear of, she reminded herself. Not like Rich at all.

But it wasn't Rich she was thinking of when she lay in bed staring at the ceiling later that night. Her thoughts were full of men with dark, shaggy hair, feverish bodies and glinting brown eyes. Stop it, she commanded herself and rolled over to stare towards the bay window at the sliver of moonlight visible through the curtains. She had expected this year to offer temptations. Overcomeable temptations—a handsome, but engaged, Will Fielding, perhaps a personable maths teacher or a witty milkman. The kinds of temptations she could easily surmount and emerge next June ready to become forever Mrs Richard Howell. Like climbing picket fences if you will. She hadn't counted on an obstacle as formidable as Mount Everest.

She hadn't expected Colin Davies at all.

CHAPTER TWO

WHEN Anna awoke the sun was streaming through the curtains and a soft breeze caressed her face. It was a luxury just to lie there and know that she hadn't a day's journey ahead of her. She had arrived.

Or had she? Suddenly last evening's events filled her mind and she groaned aloud and sat up. Far from being settled, she was on the verge of being thrown into the street. And if she succeeded in staying, might that not even be worse? Something about Colin Davies and the feelings he evoked in her made her suspect that it might be.

She dragged herself out of bed, pulling on white shorts and the same yellow T-shirt of the night before. She tugged a brush through her hair feeling decidedly grungy, and knew that the first order of the morning was a shower. Then, even if she acted like a witch when she confronted Colin Davies, she would know she didn't look like one. She got a towel from her suitcase and crept out into the hall. There was no sound from Colin's room, though the door was partly open. She didn't glance in, but instead slipped softly down the hall to the bathroom. A quick shower to wash off the miles would give her an extra bit of confidence when it finally came time to face him. And she knew she would need every ounce of help she could get.

She was under the shower, lathering her hair, when she heard the banging on the door. 'Just a minute,' she yelled. 'Hold your horses!' She screwed the cap back on the tube of shampoo and continued soaping her head. It wouldn't hurt Mr Bossy Davies to wait a few minutes. There was another loud bang and the door was wrenched open.

'Hey!' Anna poked her head out from behind the shower curtain prepared to express her annoyance in no uncertain terms, but Colin wasn't even looking at her. He knelt just inside the door, retching into the toilet. Gasping, he stopped, then leaned forward and vomited some more. Anna pulled her head back quickly and rinsed the soap out of her hair.

What now? she thought desperately. He seemed to have finished, but she hadn't heard him leave either. Mustering her courage she peeked out a second time to see him sitting hunched against the wall, his knees drawn up and his arms crossed on them, his head resting on his arms. His face was turned away from her so she could only see his untidy dark hair curling against his neck and the smooth curve of his bronze back. She licked her lips, annoyed at the reaction quickening in her. Reaching out she snatched the towel from the rack, shut off the water and began to dry off behind the curtain.

'Are you all right now?' She tried for a conversational, matter-of-fact voice that would imply that she was used to men popping in and out of the bathroom while she was taking a shower.

'Super,' he muttered, his voice hoarse. He staggered to his feet and leaned heavily on the wash basin. 'See how much easier it would have been if you'd gone to a motel instead of pushing in here?'

'I didn't push in,' she argued, sympathy vanishing. 'I was invited.'

'Not by me.'

'No, but that's not the point. I had no way of knowing you'd be here. I didn't even know you existed. What have you got against me anyway?'

'I just don't want to be bothered. The last thing I want is some pesky woman around.'

Pigheaded snot! she thought. 'Don't worry about that,' she said archly. 'I wouldn't bother you if you were the last person on earth.'

'You already *do* bother me,' he said enigmatically.

She wasn't sure she even wanted to know what he meant by that. From his tone she thought he meant more than just that she annoyed him. Her suspicions proved correct a few seconds later when he said,

'You going to stay in that shower forever?'

'Until you leave anyway.'

'I can wait.' There was a discernible leer in his tone now.

He probably could, too. And with the water shut off she was freezing. She rubbed her naked body briskly, intensely aware of her vulnerability should he decide to pull aside the curtain between them.

'You'll have a long one,' she told him, hoping that she sounded more confident than she felt. It was possible, of course, to wrap the towel sarong fashion and make a hasty exit, but she had no intention of trying it unless the house was burning down.

There was no response from Colin and she clenched her teeth together to keep them from chattering. If there were justice in the world, she thought, he would have to vomit again. It would serve him right for his perversity. Finally she heard him sigh and open the door.

'You win,' he said wearily. 'But only because I'm about to collapse. I don't know why you begrudge a sick man a little bit of pleasure. Especially as you've been nagging to live with me.'

'Don't be absurd,' she began hotly. But the door shut, and, unable to vent her annoyance on its cause, she slapped her wet wash cloth against the shower curtain, wishing heartily that it were Colin Davies's face.

She had just pulled back the curtain to step out into the mat when she heard a muffled cry and a heavy thud. Oh God! She leapt out of the bath, shouting, 'Colin!'

Wrapping the towel around her hurriedly, she yanked open the door to see Colin lying in a dead faint halfway down the hall. 'Colin!' She ran and knelt beside him. He looked deathly, his face greenish, his breathing shallow and unsteady. 'Dear God,' she muttered and ran back to the bathroom and returned with the same cold wash cloth and began gently to bathe his face with it. She couldn't move him, he was too big. Though lean he was still tall and muscular, his body rock hard and sinewy, toughened and weathered by the tropical sun. The only soft thing about him was his hair, and she brushed one hand through it now, combing it back off his forehead as she sponged his face.

At last he stirred, eyelids flickering a moment, just enough to allow her to breathe a sigh of relief. His fainting had scared her. What if she hadn't been there? How long would he have lain there before coming to and dragging himself to his bed? What if he'd hit his head? Vomited again? Choked? Her mind whirled with frightening possibilities. All of which pointed to one thing: she couldn't leave no matter what. He might not want her there (a masterful understatement), and she might know in her heart that she was better off, in terms of temptation, anywhere else, but common sense and humanitarian duty dictated otherwise, So much for all her summertime expectations. A vague dream of a happy, challenging summer spent with Will Fielding vanished without leaving a trace.

'You look very fetching in that towel,' Colin whispered now. His mouth quirked slightly. 'I got to see it after all.'

'I suppose that's why you fainted.' She glanced down at him in irritation. He knew precisely how to goad her.

'Not exactly.' He paused and managed a weak smile. 'But if this is one of the perks of fainting, I might make it a habit.' He moved his head experimentally, trying to find a more comfortable spot on her legs. 'Mmmmm. That feels good,' he murmured. 'Don't stop.'

She had been idly brushing her hand through his hair, and suddenly made aware of it by his panther-like purr, she jerked her hand away and blushed.

'Do you always do the opposite of what you're told?' he demanded, eyes suddenly piercing.

'Only with you,' she replied honestly. 'I've never met anyone like you before.' Not even Toby, she thought, and he came the closest.

'Nor I you.'

She couldn't decide then if he meant that seriously or if he was laughing at her. 'If you can get up,' she told him, 'I'll help you to your room.

'A bold act of maidenly courage,' he mocked. 'You are the most perplexing woman I have ever met. One minute you're trying to move in with me, and the next you're acting as though I'm about to ravish you. Can't you make up your mind?'

'Can't you?' she retorted. 'One minute you're throwing me out and the next you're making a pass.'

He shook his head. 'I haven't made a pass. Yet.' He grinned, and her cheeks flamed. 'When I make a pass, you'll know it.' He moved to sit up, but sank back immediately, hands going to his head. 'The damned hall spins,' he growled.

'Tough.' Anna slid out from beneath his head and stood up quickly.

'Where are you going?'

'To get dressed.'

'Leaving me here?'

'You'll manage,' she said cheekily and turned and went into her room, conscious of his glaring eyes following her every step of the way.

Damn Colin Davies anyway. Even when he was helpless as a kitten she felt at a disadvantage with him. It was ridiculous really. She was always superconfident and capable around Rich. No mumbling, no stuttering, no telltale blushes bursting forth every few minutes. No vacillating emotions. With Rich she never felt tender one moment and ready to put a dagger in his ribs the next. She had left her shorts and shirt in the bathroom, and there was no way she was going out in that hall again in her towel, so she pulled a pair of jeans and a halter top out of her suitcase and put them on. Her hair she usually left hanging free to dry, but today she thought she would look fiercer with it up, so she piled it up on her head, securing it with hairgrips and a clip, and then stood before the mirror contemplating the severity of her expression.

It was not a heartening experience. Her generous

mouth could not help curving into a smile, her freckles made her look younger than her twenty-four years, even her wide green eyes looked more mischievous than emerald hard. It was a good job she had inherited her father's quick wit and tongue, otherwise she wouldn't stand a chance with the likes of a man like Colin Davies.

He's just another dog with a sore paw, she told herself sharply. Or a pigeon with a broken wing. She was going to stay because he needed watching. And because she needed a place to live. It was a trade-off, nothing more. And if every time he looked at her she felt warm and shivery, she would just have to learn to cope with it. It would help keep her mind firmly focused on Rich.

Ah yes, Rich. He had been none too pleased at the thought of her living and working with William Fielding, even with Jenny as resident chaperon, and even though William was (his father assured her) polite, gentlemanly, and, above all, engaged. Rich would most certainly not approve of her actually living with Colin Davies who (she could personally assure him) was neither polite, nor gentlemanly, nor, if his attitude towards her was anything to go by, engaged.

It would probably be best, she decided, not to even mention the change in males. All she needed to say was that she loved the house, that Belle River was very pleasant, and that she was fine. She could get around to mentioning Colin in her own good time, when she had figured out how to explain him. If, in fact, he could be explained. But, explicable or not, he still wanted dealing with.

'Hey, come on!' she heard him yell now. 'Are you dressing for a hot date in there?'

She gritted her teeth. With one comment he could make her cheeks burn. Why did his irritating little innuendoes get under her skin that way? Anyone with three brothers ought to be immune to that sort of teasing. And when her brothers did it, she was. The trouble was, Colin Davies didn't seem brotherly at all.

'Did you say something?' she asked, coming out and standing by his feet, looking down at him stretched before her, and she smiled sweetly.

'You're gorgeous.' He grinned up at her. She felt like stepping on his chest.

'You're not,' she lied.

He affected a look of hurt outrage. 'I'll have to introduce you to all my fans.'

'That'd be an education. Is there a local branch?' She had no doubt that there would be. He looked the sort of man who left broken hearts behind him by the score.

'Oh yes. Branches all over the world.'

It figured. Definitely another Toby. Annoyed at her own inability to treat him with the indifference she would have wished for, she held out her hand. 'Come on, then, lover boy. I'll help you up.'

His calloused hand reached out to grip hers, and she slowly eased him to his feet, slipping her arm around his back and looping one of his arms across her shoulders. Calling him 'lover boy' was a mistake, she realised. It was a stupid, stupid thing to have said. It only made her more aware than ever of the fevered warmth of his body as it leaned on hers, of the mat of dark, curling hair on his chest and ribs that brushed against her hand. A purely physical reaction, she told herself as they hobbled down the hallway like a three legged monster. A reaction just like she had had with Toby. And that had certainly proved pointless.

She fairly dumped him on to his bed and stepped back immediately in order to put some space between them. But if Colin sensed that her haste was inordinate and her movements jerky, he made no comment. Rather, he eased himself carefully back against the pillows, his breath coming in short gasps again, and she realised that even that small amount of exertion had taken its toll on him. She was torn between wanting to smooth his covers and plump his pillows for him on the one hand, and getting out of there as fast as she could on the other.

'How long have you been engaged?' he asked now,

and she stared at him as though he were speaking a foreign language.

'Your ring was digging into my ribs all the way down the hall,' he explained.

'Oh.' She twisted it nervously on her finger. 'Five weeks.'

'And he let you come all the way out here?' Colin sounded enraged, more than Rich had in fact. 'What kind of spineless young puppy is he?'

'He is not a spineless young puppy,' Anna snapped. 'He's older than you are.' She would bet on that. Even ill, Colin did not look as old as Rich.

'How do you know?'

'So how old are you, Methusalah?'

'Thirty-one.'

'Rich is thirty-five.'

'And is he?'

'Is he what?'

'Rich?'

'Not especially. Why?'

'I thought that might explain why you were engaged to him.'

'Don't be ridiculous!'

He shrugged, as though his suggestion were perfectly plausible. 'Why did you get engaged then?'

Anna's teeth snapped together. 'Because I love him, obviously.'

Colin disagreed. 'Not obvious at all. Not when you're living with me.'

'I didn't know you were going to be here,' Anna argued, feeling as though she were being spun in a circle.

'William, then,' Colin said equably. 'You were going to live with him.'

'So? Rich and I are mature, independent adults.'

Colin rolled his eyes. 'Nobody's that mature,' he said flatly, and Anna wondered if he spoke from experience but didn't feel like provoking his wrath by asking.

'Perhaps *you're* not,' she said with a coolness belied by the haste with which she made for the door. His probing made her even more nervous than his sensuality did. He had without even meaning to as far as she could see, zeroed right in on her weakest spot, and she didn't like it. She wasn't even sure she liked him. He was far too arrogant, opinionated and sure of himself. Also he was far too attractive. And he took great pleasure in baiting her. She would have to pray that he got well soon and went back to Guatemala. She wasn't sure how much of Colin Davies she could take.

For the next two days she didn't have to worry about it because he kept his door firmly shut and she rarely saw him. She did watch surreptitiously from her bedroom as he staggered back and forth with the bouts of nausea that sent him to the bathroom. But he never fainted again, and the glare he gave her when he saw her watching him was enough to keep her from rushing to him and hovering like the meddlesome busy-body that he accused her of being. Unfortunately though, she didn't master the ability to pretend that he just didn't exist. She had lots of time on her hands since she had no typing or research to do for his cousin, and she spent the better part of it in a fruitless search for a job. But she was still at a loose end more often that not. And in these times she found that Colin was well on his way to becoming an obsession with her. She thought about him while leafing through magazines, while baking cakes, while reading the dry, dusty archaeological tomes and hot-off-the-press fiction she found lying around, while washing the clothes and hanging them out to dry. She made countless resolutions not to. It was like telling herself not to think about bears. Impossible. And if her mind rebelled against her dictates, her feet were just as bad. Several times a day she would find herself creeping up the stairs to Colin's room or getting off her bed if she thought she heard him making a noise. Then she would have to tell herself firmly to leave well enough alone. He doesn't want to see you, and you don't want to see him, she repeated over and over.

But she did, or at least a part of her did, and she

couldn't stop the happy lurch in her heart when he called out from his bed one afternoon, 'Anna, how about a cup of tea?'

He meant, make me one, and another time she might have told him to make it himself, but she had watched him being sick for two days without being able to offer any kind of comfort, and a cup of tea seemed like a small thing to ask. She brewed a pot and carried two cups and some date bread she had made upstairs on a tray. Not that she thought he would want a cosy conversation, but it looked cheerier than a mug and a tea bag, and cheeriness couldn't be called hovering. Besides, if he wanted her to leave, she would.

He didn't. In fact, he had straightened his sheets and cleared off a space on the dresser beside his bed for the cup. When he saw the tray he managed to smile and say, 'Even better.'

Given that mild encouragement, she stuffed another pillow behind his back and asked, 'Milk? Sugar?'

'Both, please.'

She fixed it and stirred it, then handed it to him, careful that their hands didn't touch, and he took it, not saying anything, but slanting her a mocking glance that told her that he'd noticed.

'Sit down,' he invited.

Anna looked at the rocking chair which was overflowing with books and papers and then back at Colin.

He patted the bed beside him. 'I told you before: I don't bite.'

'"Usually" you said,' Anna reminded him, but there was nowhere else to sit, so she sat. On the very edge, making the bed sag heavily and Colin's knee slid down and touched her hip. She took a sip of her tea and nearly scalded her tongue, but it gave her something to think about other than his proximity, and she tried to find something innocuous to say, but Colin spoke first.

'So tell me about this fiancé of yours,' he said, and Anna's cup rattled in the saucer.

'Why this tremendous interest in my engagement?'

she asked, sounding milder than she felt. She wished now she *had* said, make your own cup of tea.

'I'm intrigued. I don't spend every minute I'm awake thinking about Mayan ruins you know.'

'Surely you don't think about me!' she blurted, her cheeks flaming as soon as she said it, remembering all the hours she spent thinking of him.

'Why not? I mean, you burst in here unannounced, move in, make yourself at home . . .' He was grinning hugely now.

'You . . .'

'And you're so easy to bait,' he continued, 'that's why I'm curious. I've been lying here asking myself why you're engaged at all. I mean, if you're here and he's there . . .'

'And what did you decide?' She tried hard to keep her voice steady, wanting all the while to tip her teacup over his head.

'That you didn't love him.' He said it lightly enough, as though he were commenting on the weather. But the glitter in his hard, brown eyes told her that he was quite serious.

'I love him,' she replied flatly.

'Like you love your pet dog, I bet.'

'What would you know about it?' she bristled, looking away from those knowing eyes.

'I've been engaged.' He made it sound like a disease.

'Oh? I can't imagine Colin Davies being so foolish.'

'I won't be again.'

Nor would any girl, she didn't think. 'No, I imagine you won't.' she told him. 'But Rich isn't a bit like you. He's kind, gentle, dependable, caring . . .'

'Thrifty, clean and reverent. A God damn Boy Scout!' he laughed sarcastically. 'Tell me then, what does he see in you?'

Anna gritted her teeth. 'If you weren't sick, I'd smack you.'

'Touchy, aren't you?' he mocked. Then, setting his cup on the dresser, he sat up straighter. 'Show me how much you love him then,' he challenged.

'What do you mean?'

He took her cup from her hand and placed it next to his, then gently tipped her chin up, his fingers stroking her jawline. 'Tell me to stop this,' he muttered, leaning towards her, his breath fanning her cheek. 'Tell me you're totally unmoved.' His lips brushed her cheek, her temple, her eyelids, leaving kisses like flower petals warmed by the sun. And instinctively she moved towards him, delicious feelings building inside her, her hands suddenly wanting to be independent, going out to him, threading themselves in the thick, dark hair, touching him in return.

'See?' his voice rasped in her ear. 'You want me, too.'

It was like being hit with a bucket of ice cold water. Anna jerked back, aghast at what she had done. 'I don't want you,' she denied vehemently, but her hands trembled as she gripped the sheets, and the quivering in her limbs left her weak as she pulled away and stood up.

'So lie to yourself about it,' he said, his voice rough. 'But don't go on believing you're in love with this Rich character. It isn't fair to him!'

Fair? What he had done wasn't fair! What did he know about her anyway? What right had he to judge? She ran down the stairs and slammed out the front door, hoping that a brisk walk in the warm summer wind would cleanse her.

What did he know about fair? she thought furiously. Had it been fair that she had been head over heels in love with Toby Evans, thinking of marriage and three or four dark-haired, dark-eyed children, when he had been thinking of good times and bright lights and no ties at all? Had it been fair that Toby had hooked her with the ease of an expert fisherman and then had left her with the blithe explanation that he had 'other fish to fry'? No, nothing about Toby had been fair. The fairest thing that had happened to her in her whole life had been Rich Howell.

Unlike Toby he had caused no heart palpitations, no

fluttery pulse, no warm, tingly feelings. He had eased himself into her life unobtrusively. The first thing she remembered about him weren't his blond, pleasant looks or his Robert Redford smile, but his mild request, 'Two pieces of halibut, please,' which she heard every Monday for three months before he finally asked her to go out with him. He might never have done that either—the high-powered lawyer not normally looking for dates among the girls who worked in the fish shop— if he hadn't also met her at a zoning commission meeting where she was arguing with a real estate developer about protecting some low income housing from destruction. He had bailed her out with unemotional, logical arguments which had come to the aid of her emotional outburst like destroyers backing up a sampan, and when he had suggested a beer after their meeting, she hadn't any better things to do.

Not being able to think of anything better seemed to be a curse of hers at the moment. It was why she had agreed to marry him. They'd been going out steadily for over two years, she liked him, he was everything she had told Colin Davies that he was and more besides, and, above all, he made her feel emotionally safe. So when he had said, 'Will you marry me?' she thought, why not? It was only after she had the ring on her finger that the dreams started, that Toby's face cropped up again and again, and she began to wonder if it was enough with Rich to feel warm and comfortable and accustomed to his face.

She brushed her windblown hair back out of her face and stared unseeing across the cornfield she had reached at the edge of town. And now, besides memories of Toby, she had Colin Davies to deal with. From the very first moment she had seen him she had known he would be trouble. For one thing he evoked the same shivery feelings throughout her body that Toby had. 'Attracted neurons,' her mother had called it, and while her chemist brother Peter had scoffed, Anna felt that there might be something to it. She felt funny, there was no denying that. And if her physical attraction to Colin weren't enough, he had managed to attack her on her weakest point. How on earth did he know she was worried about how she felt about Rich? He didn't look the sort that was clairvoyant—his eyes were penetrating, not spacy—but no one else seemed to latch on to it the way he had. Only Teri Gibbs, her ex-roommate, had had an inkling of how she was feeling. And Teri made no bones about telling Anna she was crazy.

'If you don't want Rich, I'll take him,' she had said with a leering grin. 'For heaven's sake, what do you want? He's wonderful!'

He was. That was another of her reservations—how to live up to him. Quite apart from the fact that he didn't make her feel particularly zingy, he did make her feel inadequate. Not intentionally. It was all in her own mind and she knew it. But it was another reason she had taken this job two thousand miles away. At the end of the year she hoped to be able to go home feeling zingier for having missed him and also acting less impulsive and flighty, more the sedate, well-put-together wife that she felt a man as conscientious as Rich Howell ought to have.

And just how to accomplish that while living with Colin Davies, who not only saw all her fears and inadequacies but actually brought them out in her, she didn't know. How could he kiss her like that? She could still feel the roughness of his unshaven cheek against hers, the warmth of his lips, the brush of his eyelashes against her temple. She sank down on to the verge of the road, suddenly weak with a longing she hadn't felt since her days with Toby. She couldn't go home now, not feeling like this. Maybe by dark her sanity would have returned. She could but hope.

It was past ten when she finally felt brave enough to return. And it wasn't even really bravery that did it then so much as the conviction that he would be asleep. She had walked miles. She must have covered all the streets of Belle River more than once, but she couldn't remember a thing she had seen and hadn't the faintest idea where she had been. The house was totally dark when she got back, but she had left the door unlocked and it opened easily under her hand. Colin had been down and got himself a sandwich, the peanut butter jar was still open and a jam covered knife lay in the sink. It must have been one of his better days, she thought, aware that some of them he spent alternately shivering and burning, sweating and freezing, aching and throwing up. Maybe that was what had made him seek her company today—he felt well enough to annoy her for a change.

She washed the dishes and fixed herself a bowl of soup. She couldn't stomach anything more, and the room was so quiet she could hear herself slurping. There was enough soup for two, and another day she might have gone to Colin's room to offer him some, but not tonight. Tonight she never wanted to see him again. Maybe he had been right about Rich—maybe a marriage based on security, totally lacking in pizazz wasn't fair—but trusting one's emotions didn't seem to guarantee fairness either. Anyway, that was what the year in Belle River was supposed to help her find out. And, she told herself firmly, she could do so quite satisfactorily without the aid of Colin Davies' kisses.

Shutting out the light, she climbed the back stairs in the darkness, stopping in the bathroom long enough to brush her teeth and scrub her face before she went into her bedroom and closed the door. The moon was almost full and before midnight it shone in her room so brightly that she had no need of the overhead light to find her nightgown and slip into it. She had just lain down on her bed when she heard a tap on the door.

'Anna?'

Her stomach knotted. 'What?' She got out of bed and went to the door, opening it a crack. Colin stood leaning against the doorframe, looking down at her, but in the darkness she couldn't discern his expression. 'What?' she repeated.

He swallowed. 'I just wanted to say I'm sorry. It wasn't any of my business. And I shouldn't have kissed

you.' His voice was low but even, as though he had
rehearsed it. But if it wasn't spontaneous, it was still
shocking, and instinctively she opened the door further.

'No, you shouldn't have,' she agreed. 'But maybe I'm
especially touchy.' She didn't know why she was
confessing this in view of his just having admitted that it
was none of his business, but it seemed called for somehow.

'Are you all right? You were gone hours!' He
sounded concerned, worried, which was odd considering
that for three days he had been giving her the
impression that he wished she'd just disappear.

'I'm fine. I just went for a walk. Are you okay?'

'Yeah. It was one of my good days. Maybe it means
I'm getting well.' He grinned slightly, and she smiled
back at him like an idiot, wondering how he could
affect her like this when she'd been wishing him in hell
most of the afternoon.

'I hope so,' she told him softly, and he chuckled and
replied,

'I bet you do. The sooner I'm gone, the quicker Will
gets here and you've got a job.'

'Well, yes,' she said, but when he was like this she
didn't want to see the back of him nearly so badly.

He didn't say anything else and the silence stretched
between them awkwardly. Anna looked at her toes, pale
and bluish in the moonlight, as though they were
somehow more interesting than the muscular male body
less than six inches from her own, and Colin didn't
move away though he shifted from one foot to another.

'Am I forgiven then?' he asked, and his hand came up
as though he would touch her arm, but she looked up
quickly and it dropped to his side.

'Yes.'

'Good.' Their eyes caught and held, assessing,
curious, for once neither hostile nor awkward, and
finally he said, 'Well, g'night,' and crossed the hall to his
own room.

'Good night,' Anna whispered, but she must have
continued to stand there for a full minute after she
heard his door click shut.

CHAPTER THREE

THEY existed in an uneasy truce after that, Colin working on his notes on his 'good days' and trying to sleep through his 'bad' ones, while Anna played at housekeeping and caught up on her reading. She had given up looking for another job—there were too many college students in town who needed summer employment. She would have liked something to occupy her mind—it seemed far too full of Colin Davies—but she tried to make the best of it. Basically she avoided him, only venturing into his room to offer food or to ask a question. Only rarely did her boredom get the better of her, like the time she took him a cup of tea and perched on the edge of his bed, asking,

'What are you working on?'

He shrugged. 'A book.'

Obviously. 'On what?'

'Mayan cave painting.'

'Where? Near Tikal? Uaxactun?'

He looked at her with real interest. 'Not far from Tikal. You know about them?'

'I studied them in college,' she found herself explaining, almost apologetically. She must sound very naïve and inexperienced to someone who devoted his life to such places and knew of them first hand. 'I loved learning about them. I'd love to visit them.'

'Would you?' He looked sceptical.

'Very much. I do pottery so I was especially interested in the relics we looked at.'

'We found a fair bit,' he told her. 'I've got some sketches of some here. Do you want to see them?' His expression was doubtful, as though he expected her to refuse.

'Oh yes, please!' she said so enthusiastically that he smiled. He shuffled though his papers and handed her a stack. 'You've probably seen some like these before. But you might find some variations on designs that you're not familiar with.'

She took them eagerly, and since he didn't dismiss her as he had done often enough in the past, she settled down on the floor and began to look through them. His sketches had been done on the spot. Some of the papers were creased and smudged with dirt, but the designs were clear and deftly drawn with meticulous attention to detail. She was quite happy just to sit and look through them, picking out one or two that made her itch to reproduce them on pots of her own. She looked up to ask Colin if he minded her making copies of his drawings, not wanting to disturb him, only to find him not writing at all, but leaning back against the headboard, staring at her. His expression was unusual, hungry almost, but the moment he saw her looking at him, his features changed into a carefully schooled politeness which was only contradicted by a glint in his eye which was not so easy to disguise. Memories of his warm lips immediately took the place of her thoughts of Mayan designs, and she licked her own lips nervously.

'Would you mind if I—I mean, I'd like to, borrow these,' she fumbled, an uncomfortable warmth flooding her. Damn him for being able to do this to her with just a look.

'Go ahead,' he said easily, as though he didn't care what she did. And, flustered, she got quickly to her feet and beat a retreat to her own room, only later sneaking downstairs as though she were a common thief trying to avoid detection when all she really wanted was not to encounter him again that day.

Fortunately he seemed of a similar turn of mind, because he made no effort to come downstairs for a meal, and his light was off when she finished watching a television movie at ten and went up to bed.

The next day she didn't see him, either, but she heard him making frequent trips to the bathroom and that worried her. For all that he seemed to have some good days, he had more and more when he was violently ill.

The fifth time she heard him get up, she waited until he was staggering back to his room and met him in the hall, asking,

'Shall I call a doctor?'

He looked at her glassy-eyed and flushed with fever and shook his head. 'No doctors,' he croaked as he lurched past her and fell on to his crumpled bed. 'Just get me another blanket, will you?' She did, although the porch thermometer read 93 and the humidity was sky high. She tucked it firmly around him, and he huddled down into it like a bear going into hibernation.

'Are you sure?' she persisted, feeling brave. He looked awful, and surely it wasn't reasonable to lie there nearly dying when, as far as she knew, twentieth-century medicine hadn't even been tried.

'Don't fuss,' he mumbled into his pillow, but she couldn't help it. She idly twisted a dish towel in her hands as she watched him. Hovering, she thought grimly. He had been absolutely right about that. But what did he expect? That she would live with him for a week, argue with him, get kissed by him, and then not care what happened to him?

Rich would never expect that. When he was ill he expected her to minister to him, and he did the same for her. Very equitable. She remembered the last time he had had the flu. He had been properly grateful for the chicken soup and the clean sheets, not snapping and spilky like some people she could mention. She could use Rich now, she thought, a modicum of common sense would go a long way. Before she thought more about it she found herself in the den dialling his number.

'How are you?' she asked as soon as she heard his voice.

'Fine. What's wrong?' He expected her to call on Wednesday nights. It was Friday, and to Rich that meant trouble, not that she was missing him.

'Nothing. I just wanted to hear your voice,' she said. Sometimes over the last few days he had almost faded from her mind, so vivid were her impressions of Colin Davies. It was a good idea to have called him, she congratulated herself. Now she could see the gentle smile and the blond hair flopping across his forehead as vividly as she could usually see the harshly bearded face and dark ruffled hair of the man upstairs.

'What are you doing?' she asked him.

'Eating veal scallopini.'

Veal scallopini? On Friday? On Fridays Rich ate steak and potatoes. What was this veal scallopini business?

'Teri brought it over,' Rich explained before she could even ask.

Good old Teri. Was it an errand of mercy, Anna wondered, pity on the poor, lonely, engaged man whose fiancée had gone away? Or, she remembered Teri scoffing when she had called Rich 'safe', was she checking to see how accurate Anna's description was? Food for thought. 'How nice,' she mumbled. 'How is Teri?'

'Fine. Want to talk with her?'

Anna didn't especially. What she wanted was a nice, cosy talk with Rich that would make her feel warm and loved and that would relegate Colin Davies to the back of her mind where he belonged. But she knew immediately that it wasn't going to happen that way tonight. So she talked to Teri, and when she hung up, Rich had said, 'I love you and I miss you,' three times and Teri had promised to send her the recipe for veal scallopini, and Anna wished she hadn't bothered to call.

She spent the rest of the evening watching a western on TV that she had seen twice already, and when she went to bed, she shut the door to her room without even checking on Colin. The temptation to 'hover' was too great.

She didn't know what time she woke that night, but the heat was oppressive, smothering. She had tossed and turned for hours in the throes of very vivid dreams, first about Toby, then about Rich and Colin. But what woke her was not her own dreaming, but a sound, loud and terrible. She sat bolt upright, wide awake, Where was she? For a moment she didn't know. It was pitch dark and her disorientation was total. Then, suddenly she knew: she was at the Fieldings' and Colin Davies was just across the hall. Being murdered from the sound of it. She leapt out of bed, not bothering to grab her robe, and dashed over to his room.

The moonlight cascading through his windows outlined everything in stark silvery blue and white relief. Her eyes went immediately to the bed where Colin lay writhing and twisting. As she flung open the door he screamed again, expressions of anguish and violence chasing across his face.

'No!' he muttered. 'God, no! No!' He put up his hands to shield his face, and Anna rushed over, catching him by the shoulders and trying to wake him.

'Colin! Wake up!'

Frantic, he jerked away from her, flinging her back so that she hit her hip on the corner of the dresser and swore. How could anyone so ill be so strong?

'Colin!' She approached him again, her voice gentle this time. Urgency didn't get through to him, but maybe calmness would. 'Colin,' she repeated. 'It's all right.' There was a lie. How could anything that made him so hysterical be all right? 'Colin?'

'No! God, leave me alone!' His eyes were tightly closed, his face screwed up against unimaginable tortures. His skin burned where she touched him, not damp now, but dry and parched like a desert. She knelt beside him on the bed, holding his shoulders firmly but gently, dragging him around to face her, trying to guard against his lashing arms, saying his name over and over, praying to God that he would wake soon. After what seemed an eternity, his eyes opened, he appeared to focus on her momentarily. Then his eyes shut again and he shuddered violently.

'Colin?' Gently now. 'It's not real. It's just a dream. You're going to be all right.'

He moaned and his eyelids flickered, dazed and confused. She did see a tiny glimmer of recognition, gone almost as quickly as it had come, but it was enough for her to know that he had left the terrifying land of his dreams. He trembled, burying his face in her breasts and clinging to her, taking deep, shaking breaths. Anna rocked him, instinctively knowing how to soothe, massaging the tense cords at the nape of his neck and stroking his hair until she felt his body gradually relax against her. His weight pressed her back into the pillows, and she shifted her position so she could hold him more comfortably. It was so quiet now that she realised that not even the earliest morning birds had begun their songs. All she could hear was Colin's laboured breathing and her own hand as it stroked, feather-lightly, across his hair, neck, and back.

'Do you want to talk about it?' she asked softly after he had calmed down. 'Can you tell me what happened?'

She felt him shake his head against her. Then he whispered raggedly, 'It's all Mayan. Sacrifices. God . . .' and he shuddered again, his grip on her arms tightening. 'God.'

'Is this the first time?'

'That I've dreamed it? No. Screamed the house down? Yes.' He took a shaky breath and said, 'Sorry about that.'

'Why don't I call a doctor, Colin? You're burning up.'

He struggled up, pulling away from her, and then lay back on the bed beside her, his arms crossed under his head, eyes staring up at the ceiling. 'No,' he said, his voice remote.

She leaned on one elbow, watching him, noticing the way the shadows played off the angles and planes of his face, thinking what a strong face it was. Even in distress there was nothing weak about Colin Davies. 'Why not?' she asked.

'Just *no*,' he said, as if that were enough. My word is law and all that rot. God, what pigheadedness. Anna shook her head in despair. His jaw trembled slightly, his fever so high he was shaking, and still he didn't want a doctor. He closed his eyes, and Anna made a wry face. How could he go back to sleep so easily? Scream bloody murder one minute and drop off to sleep the next? Well, maybe he was too feverish to do anything else. Damn him anyway. If he had an ounce of sense he'd let her call a doctor. She had half a mind to do it anyway. She levered herself up carefully, trying to get off the bed without disturbing him, but his hand shot out, hot and rough, and grabbed her wrist. He rolled on to his side, eyes wide open now, searching her face.

'Stay with me,' he whispered. 'Don't go.'

Anna loked at him, wondering. It's the fever, she thought. Most of the week he's been wishing me gone, and now he's a clinging vine. 'All right,' she whispered back, touching his cheek, stroking the rough beard. 'I'll stay.'

He flung his arm around her, drawing her close and resting his head beneath her chin. It was like being wrapped up in a furnace, like wearing a fur coat on the Equator, she thought, not quite believing where she was. He shifted experimentally, then apparently found a comfortable spot, for his restlessness ceased and he sighed deeply.

Anna lay pinned to the sheet, her mind reeling. She tried to think of Rich. It seemed a safe thing to do. What would he be doing now? she wondered. She wanted desperately for her mind to wander around that topic for a while, but it was quite clear that Rich, being sensible as well as faithful, would be at home in bed asleep, alone, and no further speculation was necessary. She, on the other hand, was here, lying beneath Colin Davies, completely aware of the muscular frame sprawled across her, her nerve endings at attention from her head to her toes. She shifted uneasily, trying to feel maternal, to comfort him as she would a child—as she had, in fact, a few moments earlier when he had first awakened. But he wasn't inspiring those sensations now. Instead a warmth was spreading though her which was only partly attributable to Colin's body heat. The rest was a product of her own reaction to him. She tried to be disgusted with herself. How on earth could she let herself get into such a mess? She had come to

Wisconsin to prove herself independent and to discover how much she loved Rich. That meant learning how to stop and think, how to weigh consequences, alternatives and implications. So what was she doing lying in bed with a man who, a week ago, had been a total stranger who seemed to think that she was at worst a pest and at best an object of teasing, and to whom she was attracted more strongly than she had ever been attracted to anyone in her life. Including Toby.

God, she thought, how do I *do* these things?

She ran her hands over his bare back feeling for any sign of perspiration, anything that would indicate that the fever was breaking. There was nothing. But he felt her move and his arm tightened around her waist.

'Don't leave me, Anna,' he muttered into the folds of her nightgown, and she whispered into his hair,

'No, Colin, I'll stay right here.' She felt the tension ease in him then, as though he had for a while at least, decided to trust her. Then her head dropped to rest against his hair, soft as it touched her cheek, and she slept from sheer exhaustion.

In the morning she called the doctor. Miracle cures were for books, movies and other people. Not for Colin who had become delirious on towards morning and had awakened her as he thrashed around muttering, 'Ma! No, Ma! Don't leave me, Ma!'

Anna had held him closer, murmuring to him, all the while praying that when day broke it would be over.

'What doctor should I call?' she asked when at last he opened feverish eyes to the morning and finally knew her.

'I'm not dying,' he protested.

That was distinctly debatable, Anna thought, but she didn't say so. She reached over and smoothed the hair off his damp forehead, and he caught her hand and held it against hot, trembling lips. Instinctively she moved to withdraw it, her emotions jolted and confused, but he hung on fiercely, so she left it where it was though the sensation of his lips caressing her palm sent shivers down her spine.

'Anna?' Fever bright eyes bored into hers.

'Hmmm?'

'You win. Call Whitmeyer. He lives right down the street.'

Hallelujah, she thought. Sanity at last. But she just nodded and pressed her fingers lightly against his lips. 'I will,' she promised. 'Rest now. It'll be all right.

'Hospital,' Dr Whitmeyer decreed, concern written on his ruddy, bespectacled face as he stood by Colin's bed and contemplated his patient. Anna wilted with relief, glad that she had called him. He had come on his lunch hour and had wasted no time in telling Colin he had been a fool.

'You should have know better,' he said now, shaking his head at the obvious stupidity of those who procrastinate before calling their physicians. 'You've neglected this far too long.'

'I know what it is. I've had it before,' Colin protested.

'Exactly. All the more reason to get it seen to immediately.' Dr Whitmeyer tapped his pencil impatiently on the dresser. 'Rest is fine as far as it goes. In your case it doesn't go far enough.'

'I have to go back to Guatemala,' Colin argued. He hauled himself up against the pillows and glared at the doctor.

Dr Whitmeyer wasn't fazed. 'I understand that. You should be able to go by September if you behave now. At the earliest.'

Colin flinched at the words. 'September?' He looked aghast. 'I have to go in a couple of weeks. And I teach for Will starting Monday.'

Dr Whitmeyer looked at Anna and seemed to say with his eyes that he wished he were anywhere else. 'You'll still be in the hospital Monday.'

Anna could almost see the wheels spinning in Colin's head as he frantically searched for a way out of his dilemma. As far as she could see, though, there wasn't one. And apparently he couldn't find one either for he

sagged defeatedly against the pillows and when Dr
Whitmeyer said,

'I'll drop you by the hospital after lunch,' Colin
didn't even bother to answer, just shut his eyes and
turned his head to the wall.

'Be back in half an hour,' Dr Whitmeyer said to
Anna. 'Can you have him ready?'

'Yes.' A bold-faced lie if there ever was one. Colin
would be ready if he wanted to be. If he didn't, Anna
certainly couldn't make him. But a business-like
attitude might go a long way towards helping, so she
found him clean clothes and dumped them on the bed
for him, asking as she did so, 'Want any help?' knowing
that he wouldn't.

'No,' he said faintly. Then a tiny quirk appeared in
the corner of his mouth, as though something had just
struck him funny. 'I'll manage,' he said, and Anna
grinned.

When Dr Whitmeyer returned Colin was downstairs
on the sofa, fully dressed and with his hair combed, but
looking white and drained with the effort.

'All set?' Dr Whitmeyer asked.

'Mmmm,' Colin mumbled, but he made no move to
get up, just sat looking at Anna, his eyes dark and
unreadable. The look went deeper than words, touching
Anna's soul with a longing so fierce that something hurt
far down inside her, and she got to her feet.

'Come on,' she said, going over to him. 'I'm coming too.'

Nurses whisked Colin away from her before he had
even finished registering, and Anna was left with a pile
of forms to fill out. Colin had looked panic-stricken
when three of them swooped down on him, not that
Anna could blame him. Their efficiency was positively
frightening. Hers, by comparison, was positively
non-existent. Having to fill in blanks about Colin's life
told her quite clearly how little she really knew about
him. Will or Jenny would have to give them more
information later. Giving up, she handed the forms
back to the registrar and was directed upstairs.

Colin's door was firmly shut, and when she tapped

tentatively on it, another paragon of efficiency dressed in white popped out just long enough to say, 'He's gone to sleep. Come back later,' and shut the door in her face.

So much for being needed. But she had promised him she would 'stay with him', even if the promise meant nothing to him now that medical help was here, it still meant something to her. Even if it meant 'staying' out in the hall.

She busied herself by calling Jenny Fielding at the house where she was visiting, telling her about what was happening. Jenny sounded delighted that Anna had come and amazed that Colin was hospitalised ('You mean he let them? He must be dying!') and sounded basically as welcoming and unthreatening as Anna had hoped she would. She was, however, worried about who would teach on Monday. Anna hadn't given it much thought until now, but at Jenny's persuasion she agreed to try and get hold of Will. That accomplished, she went back to the visitor's lounge and poured herself a cup of stale coffee while she tried to figure out how to get a message to William in the outer reaches of Guatemala. Footsteps clicked down the hall, trolleys rattled by, and the low drone of voices lulled her into a sleepy stupor. She felt as wrung out as the dish rag she had used on the kitchen worktops that morning. Nodding, she closed her eyes.

'Miss Douglas?' a voice penetrated her consciousness. Anna blinked. A stout, fiftyish woman, looking like a well-filled milk bottle in her white uniform trouser suit, was standing over her.

'Yes?'

'Mr Davies is asking for you. We thought you'd left but . . .'

'I never!' Anna protested, jumping to her feet. She followed the nurse quickly back down the hall, trying to straighten her clothes and hair.

'You must try to convince him to sleep,' the nurse said. 'He's very upset. Just get him to relax. He will for you.'

Not likely, Anna thought, but she pushed the door open and went in alone. It might have been a total stranger lying there, an alien being, caged and trussed. Metal sides fenced him in, intravenous bags dripped unknown substances into his arm. Her throat closed and the bottom fell out of her stomach. She wanted to turn and run, but at the sound of her footsteps he turned his head and green eyes met brown ones. Suddenly he was no stranger, and, mesmerised, she walked towards the bed.

'They said you'd left,' he whispered, struggling to sit up.

'No. They wouldn't let me in before. I was down the hall.' She touched his arm, pressing him back, and he acquiesced, lying down again.

'Oh.' Her answer seemed to satisfy him, and she was doubly glad she had bothered to stay. A small thread of trust seemed to exist between them at last. She reached out and touched his hand and his fingers curled instinctively around hers. Just how long she sat there with him she wasn't sure. Dinner came and went. So did a whole shift of nurses. Dr Whitmeyer poked his head in about eight-thirty on evening rounds and looked amazed.

'Still here?' he asked, and Anna nodded.

The only time she left him was to try and contact William, not an easy business since direct dialling did not extend to the Guatemalan jungle. At last she sent a telegram and called Jenny back to tell her what she had done. Jenny seemed pleased and promised to come to the hospital in the morning to visit Colin. She also promised to move back home immediately, which made Anna feel immeasurably more cheerful when she went back to Colin's room. Somebody would be in the big house when she got there, somebody would get the telegram to William, somehow it would all work out.

She managed her first real smile of the day when the night nurse came out of Colin's room and said, 'He's doing better dear. How about a nice cup of tea?'

'Sounds terrific.'

'I'll bring you one.'

Marvelling at a nurse who considered it her job to take care of the visitors as well as the patients, Anna sank into the chair next to Colin's bed dozing until the nurse appeared, cup in hand.

'My fiancé was wounded in Vietnam,' she confided when Anna offered her a grateful smile. 'I never left him either when they sent him home.'

'Oh,' Anna said numbly, knowing that the nurse had seen her ring and jumped to the wrong conclusion. She ought to explain, she thought, but she was too tired. And what did it matter anyway? So she just sipped the tea and said, 'Thank you very much,' and smiled again as the nurse patted her arm before she went away.

The night was very much like the day had been. As the sedatives wore off Colin awoke more frequently, eyes searching, hand groping, until she held it firmly again. On towards morning, when he seemed more deeply asleep, she collapsed herself, totally drained, into the chair by the bed and tucked an extra blanket around her. Just another night of staying up with a stray puppy, she thought sleepily, or an injured cat. But then, just as sleep overcame her, she remembered his expressive brown eyes and warm lips, the strength of his arms around her, and she knew quite clearly that it wasn't the same at all.

When she woke up she felt as though she had been bent by an incompetent pretzel maker. All the kinks and bends were in the wrong directions. 'Erggg,' she groaned, unbending slowly, aware suddenly of where she was and of the deep brown eyes fastened on her face.

'Good morning,' she croaked, wishing that her sleepy huskiness was not quite so obvious. She felt very vulnerable knowing that he had been watching her sleeping. How long had he been awake anyway?

'Good morning,' he replied with a slight smile. There was a bit of colour in his cheeks again, and his eyes were alert, not bright with fever as they had been. She knew he must be cooler, but she didn't dare reach out a hand to feel his forehead to be sure. He was watching her interestedly, with neither the hostility nor the mocking that she had met so often during the past week.

'You look very nice when you're asleep,' he offered finally, and she replied,

'So do you!' which, the moment she said it embarrassed her so thoroughly that she wanted to drop through the floor. But Colin didn't seem to mind in the least.

He grinned lopsidedly. 'I'm glad to hear it,' he said, and the slightly mocking tone returned to his voice. Then his face went serious and he said, 'Thanks. For staying, I mean.'

Anna ducked her head, trying to hide the confusion she felt. 'You're welcome.'

'You must be exhausted.'

'I'll manage,' she said, and couldn't help grinning. Colin laughed. 'How are you feeling?' She went on. 'It's you we're worried about.'

'Not too bad. Weak as a kitten though. I wonder if this is a good patch or if I've really turned the corner.'

'Oh, I would think you're on the mend,' she said quickly, sensing how desperately he needed some encouraging words. 'But that doesn't mean you can get the next plane back to Guatemala,' she cautioned.

'Probably not. But I do feel better.' He shifted on to his side and lay with his head on his arm, just looking at her. She looked back, noting the definite improvement in both his looks and temperament, but beginning to feel distinctly uncomfortable again under the scrutiny of his gaze. It was too intimate, and finally, nettled and unnerved by his minute observation, she asked,

'Do you approve?'

A wicked grin lit his face, enchanting and astonishing her. She had never seen him look like that before. It did disastrous things to her heart. If he had been attractive when he was nearly dead, brooding and grim, he was devastating now. 'You know I do,' he reminded her with a leer that made her flush to the roots of her hair. She stood up hastily and shuffled around trying to slip her shoes back on.

'I'm delighted to know you feel so much better,' she said stiffly, dredging up a mental image of Rich. 'I think I'll go on home then.'

'Chicken,' he said softly, which flustered her even further, and she grabbed up the pile of magazines she had been reading earlier and held them in front of her in a flimsy defensive gesture that only seemed to amuse him more.

'Goodbye.' She turned to dash for the door.

'Anna!' His voice changed now, the teasing quality replaced by a sudden urgency. She looked back to see him propped on one elbow, struggling to sit up. 'When will you be back?'

The quick switch baffled her. How could he act like a wolfish mocker one moment and a lonely little boy the next? How on earth could she relate to someone like that? She thought again of Rich. With Rich there were no abrupt switches, no surprises, and never any question of what to say next. Rich went through life with a well-written script, and with him Anna unfailingly knew her lines. With Colin, it seemed, the opposite was true—life was an exercise in improvisation.

'I'll be here at noon,' she promised. 'Okay?'

'Yeah.' He nodded and lay back down, but Anna still sensed a tension in him, and she crossed back over to stand beside the bed.

'If you want anything, call. They'll be hooking up your phone this morning. Jenny will answer if I don't. She's moving home today.' She gave him a quick smile, feeling rather like a mother leaving her child on the first day of school, and then surprised herself as much as him when she bent suddenly and brushed her lips on his forehead. Without another word, she turned and fled.

* * *

She didn't think about that last scene in the hospital
again. Some things were better left undissected, and this,
Anna was sure, was one of them. Besides, when she got
back to the house she had enough to worry about.

'Somebody called Rich rang up last night,' Jenny told
her.

'Oh heavens. What did you tell him?'

'Just that you'd taken my cousin to the hospital.
Why? Did I say something wrong?' Jenny answered,
seeing Anna's stricken expression.

'Oh, no. No,' Anna assured her. 'Is that all? What did
he say?'

'Just that you hadn't mentioned any cousin. Who is he?'

'My fiancé,' Anna explained. 'I didn't think he'd
want to hear about Colin.'

Jenny reflected on this a moment and then said, 'He
was willing to have you stay here with Will and me.'

'Not quite the same thing,' Anna said drily.

Jenny grinned. 'I guess not. Colin's definitely more
dangerous than Will.'

Anna thought so too. Particularly where she was
concerned. From the standpoint of magnetism and
sheer sexual attractiveness Colin Davies was probably
one of the most dangerous men she was ever likely to
meet. 'You can see, then, why I didn't mention the
circumstances of the last week to Rich,' she said.

'I see. Anyway,' Jenny brightened. 'Will called too.
He'll be in on the nine o'clock flight to Dubuque
tonight. So Rich will never know the difference. It'll be
you and Will and me, just as if Colin had never come.'

But Colin had come, and nothing Anna said or
pretended would change that. Rich might never know
about the past week, but Anna was always going to be
different because of it. She couldn't imagine now a
world without Colin Davies in it. Like it or not he was
a real part of her existence. Just what part, she wasn't
sure. Frankly she was scared to find out.

Damn it, she thought, I love Rich. He is kind, steadfast
and lovable. He's all I'll ever need. So what good was this
ridiculous feeling of attraction to Colin anyway?

CHAPTER FOUR

ANNA was still worrying it over, like a dog with a bone, all the way to Dubuque that evening. She had spent two hours in the afternoon watching Colin sleep. He had awakened briefly, making no more mocking remarks, content simply to hold her hand, and she couldn't take her eyes off him. Whatever the attraction was, it was undeniably real. And she would have to find a way to deal with it. For a moment she thought that telling him she was going to pick up William would do it. She expected such a furious reaction that she would be only too glad to get away from him, but it didn't work out that way. She saw less anger in his face than a sense of failure, and she knew he could see his Guatemala project slipping away right before his eyes. With Will back in the States, the work would come to a virtual standstill. Colin had told her before about having to contend with looters, and she knew that was what worried him now. The pain she saw in his eyes stabbed her, and she squeezed his hand tightly, but there was nothing at all that she could say.

William Fielding was everything she had been expecting. No surprises here—just a tall, masculine version of Jenny, the same straw-coloured hair and spattering of freckles, the same engaging grin. In it she could even see a faint echo of Colin's and her heart momentarily quickened. If he didn't surprise her, she was apparently just what he had been expecting too. He came up to her immediately and offered his hand.

'Hi. I'm Will. You're Anna? How's Colin?'

She smiled. 'Better. Except for hearing you were coming.'

'Figures.' He grinned. 'Too bad it didn't work out like we'd planned. This was his expedition, you know.'

Anna nodded, remembering that Colin had said that

it was with the fierce pride of a parent when talking about his own child. She lifted the second of his two duffle bags and led him out to her car.

'It was sheer bad luck, him getting this bug,' Will went on. 'None of the rest of us got it. I suppose he forgot his pills or something. When does Whitmeyer think he'll be able to go back?'

'September or later.'

Will whistled. 'Bad news. Between the precariousness of the political situation and the looters he'll be lucky if there's anything left by September.' He folded himself into the VW and sighed. 'How about stopping for a hamburger? I'm starved. Six months in the jungle always gives me a taste for junk food.'

He directed her to a fast food restaurant, and over hamburgers and milk shakes she found herself describing the past week to him. She might have known him for years. In personality, he could have been a clone of her brother, Peter—the same dry wit, ability to listen, and a large store of common sense. If he'd come home as planned, she knew she'd never be wracked by all the tumultuous thoughts that plagued her now. The week would have been easy and straightforward with William.

'He should be grateful you were brave enough to bully him into calling Whitmeyer,' Will was saying. 'He was a damn fool not to call a doctor right away. But he always did have a thing about doctors and hospitals.'

'What do you mean?'

'Well, most kids don't like 'em. Don't myself. But Colin was always beyond the pale. When we were about 12 he cut his leg badly. Needed stitches. I thought he was going to literally fight my mother about taking him to the hospital. He kept saying, "No. They can't make me stay. I won't stay!"' Will took a long swallow of his milk shake. 'I remember the tone of his voice—sheer panic. Really out of character for Colin. He was a tough kid, nothing scared him. But he was shaking over that. And it wasn't the cut; it was the hospital.'

Anna nodded. Will had reconfirmed everything she

had felt whenever she mentioned doctors or hospitals to Colin. She was even more glad that she hadn't just left him and gone home. Whatever he didn't like, at least she had been there to share it.

'Did he say why?' she asked.

'Good God, no. He's very well defended, our Colin. A good man, but he doesn't let anyone inside the walls.' He grinned at her over the top of his glass. 'Or had you noticed?'

'I had.'

'Thought so.' He finished his hamburger and wiped his mouth. 'I guess we'd better be getting on. I wouldn't mind hitting the sack. It's hard to believe that this morning I woke up in a little *posada* about 100 years and fifteen kilometres removed from the twentieth century.' He stood up and guided her out of the restaurant. 'Nice to be home,' he said, stretching.

'I hope so,' Anna said doubtfully.

'Oh, it is. Teaching is great balance for field work. I like it a lot. It's Colin who prefers the field.'

'He's devoted to his work, I'll give him that,' Anna said. 'He hung on to it to the bitter end.'

'He would. I think he trusts facts on paper and people who've been dead for thousands of years more than he trusts the rest of us,' Will said. 'Likes them better too. But,' he grinned, 'it doesn't stop him from having a damned good time when he wants to!'

'I'd gathered that,' Anna said, remembering that she'd thought he looked like the sort who'd been around.

'Well, it's enough for him,' Will said. 'He was engaged once. A bad business. Since then his work has been everything he's needed. And frankly I don't reckon he'd find many women who'd want to trek through the jungle after him even if he decided he did want to settle down. Which he doesn't.'

Shades of Toby, Anna thought. Another Mr No-commitments just as she had suspected. Oh God, she uttered a silent prayer, why can't you just let me hate him. It'd be so much easier.

'You're settling down though, I hear,' she changed the subject.

'Yes. Andrea is a botanist who doesn't mind jungles. She looks at the flowers and I look at the dirt. We make an interesting pair.'

'You miss her.' It wasn't a question. Anna could hear it in his voice.

'God, do I! We were both so wrapped up in our work that it didn't seem psssible we'd even miss each other this year. But I feel lost half the time, as though some part of me is missing.'

'Tell me about her,' Anna urged, and he did. All the way back to Belle River Will talked. And Anna heard more than she'd thought was possible—not just about Andrea either. She heard about William too—and she heard in the depths of her being, something about herself. A tiny voice told her just how much she was missing Rich Howell, and compared to how much Will was missing Andrea, it wasn't much at all.

Once Will was home and working it seemed hard to believe that the week with Colin alone had ever existed. Swamped with last-minute class preparations and intent on getting started on writing up his own notes, Will pressed Anna into service immediately. Her knowledge of Spanish and her pottery experience were just the pluses that Professor Fielding had predicted they would be, and by Friday Will was delighted and Anna was exhausted. Colin was obviously not the only one in the family dedicated to his work.

But Will was a considerate boss, and his unfailing good humour made Anna willing to go the extra mile to help him out. She spent hours helping him by filing, typing, translating, and even once, piecing together a tricky bit of a pot. She enjoyed it immensely, and she took her enthusiasm with her when she went to talk to Colin who didn't appreciate it at all.

It seemed to her that he became increasingly irritated every time she told him what she and William had been doing. He practically jumped at her with questions the moment she walked in the room, and then seemed to do nothing but find fault with her answers. Especially those which involved her work with William.

'God,' he muttered once. 'You'd think he was a damn movie star the way you go on about him.'

'I just said that I liked helping him,' Anna protested. 'What do you care?'

'I don't,' he snapped, and proceeded to ignore her, looking out the window at a garbage truck instead with such avid interest that she could cheerfully have wrung his neck.

Noting that his irritation seemed to increase directly in proportion to how much she mentioned Will and her work for him, Anna soon stopped talking about that at all. But then there was nothing to say. Colin wasn't the sort you made small talk with, so they would sit and stare into space or at the walls in awkward silences until she would resolve that the next day she wouldn't bother to come. But every time she got up to leave he would say quickly, 'When will you be back?' as though it mattered. So she always came.

The visits were increasingly torturous to her peace of mind. She would have liked to have forgotten him, and when she was busy working for Will, she did. But then, every day after work, she would trek back to the hospital and all the events of their week together would come crowding in on her again. How on earth she would cope when Colin got out of the hospital and they were living in the same house again, she didn't know. She didn't dwell on it either. When it happened there would be time enough to panic then.

The time came sooner than she thought. A week after Colin was admitted, she and Will stopped by his room to find Dr Whitmeyer beaming at his much improved patient.

'It's all right with me,' he was saying. 'You can go provided that they're willing to put up with you at home.'

Colin looked warily from Will to Anna and back

again as if trying to gauge their response. Finally Will asked, 'What do you mean "put up with"?'

'He's going to want watching,' Dr Whitmeyer explained. 'Slowing down. We've practically tied him down as long as he's been here. If he goes home now and tries to pick up where he left off, I can guarantee he'll be back in the hospital within a week.'

'But I——'

'I know you don't feel bad,' he interrupted Colin. 'But you haven't got the strength of a newborn baby. You have got to take it easy, full stop.'

Anna thought that Colin's looks certainly belied the doctor's words. Clean-shaven and attractive, even in hospital issue pyjamas, he was a far cry from the man who had entered the hospital a week ago. Every day had seen an improvement, and she knew he had been badgering the doctor since Tuesday, the first day he had kept down solid food and managed to walk to the bathroom without passing out, to let him come home. She knew also that Dr Whitmeyer had not been easy to convince. So if he thought it was all right now, she guessed it must be.

'What do you think?' Will asked her, 'Shall we?'

Anna's stomach churned. It might be all right for Colin, she thought, but it was definitely going to be dangerous for her.

'Anna won't mind,' Colin said, grinning. 'She's seen me at my worst. She knows I'm bound to get better, don't you, Anna?' He flashed her the same teasing grin that always caused her to wish the floor would swallow her up.

'Oh, uh, yes,' she fumbled, striving for a light tone. 'You could hardly act worse.' I hope, she thought.

'There. See,' Colin said, triumphant.

'After lunch then. Home and straight to bed,' Dr Whitmeyer said.

'Fine, we'll see to it,' Will replied.

'I'd rather Anna did,' Colin said, giving her a sideways glance that caused Dr Whitmeyer to raise an eyebrow and Anna's blush to deepen.

'I am not your nurse!' she said fiercely.

'Really? You certainly wanted to be last week,' he teased.

'Only because you were too stubborn and pigheaded to get yourself to a doctor!'

Dr Whitmeyer looked like he was watching a tennis match until he recollected where he was and broke in, 'Another thing: my patient should not become excited. It will slow his recovery.'

Colin grinned smugly. Anna glared. How dare he? How like Toby he was! Quite willing to sit there all handsome and smiling, teasing and flirting, quite without scruples. Now that he was feeling better he seemed very eager to make her part of the 'good time' Will said he was so fond of. It looked as though her worries were well-founded. She would have to work hard on holding out against his charm. The first step would be to find somewhere else to be this afternoon when Will brought him home.

No such luck as it turned out.

'I've got a department meeting,' Will announced at lunch. 'And Jenny's babysitting.' So Anna went to get him herself. But if she feared his strength of personality, she soon learned that, at the moment anyway, she had nothing to worry about in terms of his strength of body. He was, just as Dr Whitmeyer claimed, too weak to do anything.

Except attract Anna. She was beginning to think he'd have to be dead before he stopped doing that. Her VW had never seemed smaller than when he was sitting in it. His presence, even silent, simply overpowered her, and she thought, I've got to talk to Rich tonight. She had been avoiding it all week, not wanting to talk about Colin Davies to him, but now, faced with the man in question, talking to Rich had never seemed like a better idea.

By the time she had Colin upstairs she was shaken and breathless. I've been working too hard, she thought as she escaped to the kitchen. But she knew that wasn't entirely the reason. A very large part of it was directly

attributable to her proximity to Colin Davies. She had
had to hold him up all the way from the car through the
kitchen and up the back steps, stopping to rest
whenever he had looked ready to collapse. And just the
feel of his body against hers had set off tremors in her
that should never have existed. When she finally
dropped him on the bed, she was shaking as badly as he
was. To recover her equilibrium she had started out,
saying, 'I'll bring you something to drink,' only to
receive a further shock to her system when she returned
to find him stripping down to his underwear before
getting under the sheet.

'Don't mind me,' he said, grinning faintly at her
shocked expression. 'Anyway,' he said, stretching out
and folding his arms beneath his head, 'as you're
engaged, you've undoubtedly no reason to be shocked.'

Anna almost blurted that she and Rich had never . . .
But she thought that, knowing Colin, he would either
disbelieve her or would simply laugh at her innocence,
so she stood helplessly, staring at him, wishing she had
the strength of mind to look away, until he said,
'Would you like to put that glass on the table?' in such
an infuriatingly calm tone, that she suddenly came to
life, thumped it on the table, and bolted for the door,
saying over her shoulder,

'Call if you need anything.' She flew down the stairs
as if goblins were after her. It didn't help at all to hear
him laughing.

She was doing the dishes when the 'phone rang that
evening. She had been waiting for it as eagerly since
that afternoon as she had been avoiding it earlier in the
week. Rich had called almost every night, and every
night she had been at the hospital. But the moment of
truth had arrived. She couldn't avoid talking about
Colin Davies any longer.

'You're always out,' he said, almost the first thing.
'Where on earth do you go every night. And who's this
cousin in the hospital? What's he have to do with you?'

He sounded annoyed, and Anna thought he was not
going to understand at all. It would be best just to stick

to the facts. The barest, most minimal facts. 'It's Dr Colin Davies,' she said. 'He's the head of the expedition that Will—er, Dr Fielding—was on. He got malaria and some other disease and he's come up to stay with the Fieldings. I've just been visiting him since Will and Jenny are very busy.' It was the truth, she thought defensively. And what's more, it was exactly the sort of thing Rich was used to her doing.

'Oh, another injured seagull?' Rich sounded amused. 'Is he still in the hospital?'

'No. He came home today. Now we're taking care of him till he can go back to Guatemala.'

'Good.'

'Good?'

'Yes. I never did think a fifteen-year-old girl was an adequate chaperon for you and that William Fielding. I'm glad this Dr Davies is there to keep an eye on things.'

Anna nearly choked.

'I expect you'll take good care of him,' Rich went on. 'Just think of him as another stray dog. You do take them all in.'

'Dr Davies is not exactly a stray dog,' Anna laughed, wishing he was there to hear himself so described.

'The principle is the same: stray dogs, injured seagulls, cats hit by cars, archaeologists with malaria. I should be glad, I suppose,' Rich said philosophically. 'It keeps you out of trouble.'

'I didn't know you thought I was inclined to get into trouble,' Anna said stiffly. She felt perilously close to arguing with Rich, something she had never done before. She was emotionally much too finely tuned at the moment, and it wouldn't take much to set her off.

Rich apparently realised this for he said. 'I don't. I just miss you. Why the hell did you have to go anyway?' It was the first time he had really expressed any anger at her decision and it surprised her. It also increased her guilty feelings.

'It seemed like a good idea at the time,' she said helplessly. It didn't seem so great right now. Now she would have liked nothing better than to turn back the clock and be in Los Angeles with nothing more complicated to think about than what she would wear on a date with Rich that night. She did not want to face sorting out her emotions about Rich Howell and Colin Davies.

'I went to a party at Ed Jamison's the other night,' Rich told her. 'You'd have enjoyed it.' He went on to talk about the bash at Jamison's lavish 'Tudor ranch' in Palos Verdes, and Anna found herself thinking, That's the night I sat until dawn in the hospital, and she knew she didn't regret missing the party at all. Only because I'm not a party person, she told herself hastily.

'It sounds like it was fun,' she replied. 'I do miss you, Rich.'

'Good. Why don't you just come home?'

'I can't. I don't break contracts.'

He sighed. 'All right. But keep on missing me. And take care of all those strays. Even this Davis person . . .'

'Davies.'

'Whatever. Just keep away from Fielding.'

If you only knew, Anna thought, but she said, 'Yes. Call me Sunday?'

'Of course. Don't drop any bedpans. And be nice to the old chap.' Rich hung up and Anna felt guiltier than ever. She should have told him that Colin Davies was seventeen times more attractive to her than Will Fielding would ever be. But she hadn't because the feelings she felt for Colin were like those she'd felt for Toby—only worse. And no one knew better than she did that those sorts of feelings weren't enough at all.

She had met Toby Evans at a fraternity party her second year at UCLA. She had only gone because her roommate, Lorraine, was engaged to one of his fraternity brothers. She had been sitting in a corner like a lump, wishing she'd gone to the library to study for her history mid-term exam, when she had looked across the room and had seen Toby. He was undoubtedly the most devastating man she had ever seen and she promptly fell head over heels. It was insane, really, that instant attraction, she told herself later when she was capable of doing post-mortems on their relationship. She should never have smiled so broadly, never have danced so close, never have listened to all those words he said and that she so desperately wanted to hear. But she had, and in no time she and Toby Evans were an item.

They double-dated with her engaged friends, they took long moonlit strolls on the beach, they did some serious necking in his Triumph sports car. It was lucky, she thought afterwards that he'd had a Triumph. In anything more accommodating considerably more than their necks and related anatomical parts would have been involved! She had always thought she would want to wait for marriage to completely share herself with a man, but Toby had blinded her good sense. He was in her every waking thought and all her dreams. He was her future, and she would have given him whatever he wanted had the opportunity arisen. Thank God it had not.

Her first hint that she was not to Toby what he had become to her were friends' comments about his escapades. 'He's a ladies' man,' Lorraine said. 'Darrell says he's famous for it.' But Anna brushed it off. After all, Toby was gorgeous with his mop of black hair, those piercing brown eyes, and that well-muscled body. If he had had other women in the past, that's just what they were—past. None of it mattered now that he had her. He also, according to Lorraine, had a redhead, but when Anna dared to ask him, Toby said she was his sister. Of course Anna believed him. Naïve was her middle name.

But then he missed one date, then another, forgot to call when he said he would, and called her Gloria when he kissed her. 'Who's Gloria?' she had asked, drawing away like a wounded doe.

Toby grinned, shrugging with endearing boyish embarrassment. 'Sorry, I meant to say "Anna". Gloria's a girl I used to know.'

Gloria was, Anna found out three weeks later,

expecting a baby. Lorriane said that Darrell said that Gloria said that Toby was the father. Toby laughed. Anna didn't see anything particularly funny.

'Is it true?' she asked him, feeling less hurt than horrified.

Toby shrugged again. It was, Anna was realising, his standard response. His warm brown eyes seemed inordinately cold. 'Who knows? Gloria knew what she was getting. It's her responsibility.'

After that there was no deceiving herself. Her dream of spending the rest of her life as Mrs Toby Evans met a bitter end. 'I don't think we'd better see each other any more, Toby,' she had told him, even then trying to phrase it gently so as not to hurt him.

She needn't have bothered. 'That's okay.' He was smiling, his expression nonchalant. 'I have a job offer in Minneapolis. I leave on Tuesday.' Which he had done, and Anna was left to deal with the pieces of her broken dreams.

For a long time she hadn't dated at all, not willing to trust her judgment, afraid that any man she found attractive was going to be just as unreliable as Toby. And then, almost a year later, she met Rich. Unlike Toby he didn't make the strings of her heart zing, but she liked him—more and more as time went on. He was calm, predictable, and she soon learned that, while he might not sweep her off her feet, at least his own were planted firmly on the ground. After the mercurial, undependable Toby this was a plus indeed. For the past two years their relationship had grown from casual dating to a regular commitment. Marriage was the inevitable outcome. Rich, Anna knew, was ready to get married. It was a good time now that his career was established. He wanted to start a family before he got much older. It was all cut-and-dried and Anna was part of his pattern. She went along with it, too, because it promised her everything she thought she wanted—a man who loved her, a family, a home—with none of the risks she'd found with Toby.

Then, when the ring was on her finger, the doubt set

in. And the flickering sparks of doubt she had first felt were fast being fanned into roaring flames by her attraction to Colin Davies.

'I think we need a night out,' Will said a few days later as he and Colin and Anna watched a baseball game on TV.

'Good idea,' Colin said, his attention distracted as he began flipping watermelon seeds into Will's mother's cut glass bowl.

'Not you,' Will said. 'Just Anna and me. A night for the staff, so to speak. To get away from the patient.'

'Thank you very much.' Colin's voice was dry. 'You'll be monopolising my nurse's time.' He had taken to referring to her as his nurse because he knew it annoyed her. But the description was an apt one—she had been fetching, carrying, changing linens, taking temperatures, and doing other assorted bits of dirty work for days. Colin bent closer to get a good aim. 'She's engaged, remember?' he reminded Will off-handedly.

'So am I,' Will said. That's what makes it all right. Andrea wouldn't care and Rich wouldn't either.'

This was not precisely true, but Anna wasn't going to contradict him. She needed a night out. All week long she had been trying to remain indifferent to Colin, and while she thought she had carried it off fairly well, not giving herself away, it had been a terrific strain. She kept having to walk out of rooms she would rather have stayed in, ended conversations she would rather have continued, and ignored double-edged comments from Colin that were designed to let her know he was attracted to her. So she gave Will an enthusiastic smile and said, 'Whatever you have in mind, I'm for it.'

'I wish you'd give me encouragement like that,' Colin grumbled.

'Where are we going?' Anna asked Will, trying to ignore Colin's mutterings.

'Some of the faculty and staff are having a picnic on Eilers' farm tomorrow night. Sound good?'

'Great!'

'Where's that?' Colin asked idly.

'Near Salty's. Where we went arrowhead hunting when we were kids.'

'Oh.'

Anna looked at him, but he seemed completely absorbed in the game. She allowed her gaze to linger longer than she normally would. But when she noticed Will watching her she jerked her head around quickly and stood up. 'I think I'll finish typing those notes you gave me this morning,' she said to Will, 'and then go to bed.'

'Okay.' He gave her a relaxed smile, 'Good night.'

' 'Night,' Colin mumbled as though she were of no more interest than the wall.

Anna mounted the stairs puzzled. One minute he was all but making a pass at her, the next he seemed totally indifferent. What a pain the man was! She never knew what to expect. It would be lovely to go out for an evening and forget all about him. Rich wouldn't like her going with Will whom he saw as a threat. But she knew that, where she was concerned, Will was as safe as houses compared to his fierce, attractive cousin.

She had no time to puzzle over his behaviour though. Will kept her busy all the following afternoon putting some notes in order for him, and Colin, fed up with staying in the house, had arranged to go down to Salty's farm for the day.

'It won't kill me,' he told Anna when she protested. 'I'm fine. I can sit on his porch and shoot the bull with him as well as I can lie on this damn bed another day and read these twenty-year-old *National Geographics*.'

Anna wasn't wholly convinced though until she actually met Salty. The Special Collections librarian at the University, he was a small, grey-haired man who reminded Anna of a terrier. He had hustled Colin into his old Chevy as though he were a doting father, his concern for Colin quite evident. Anna was comforted, and when Salty said, 'I'll take care of him now,' Anna was sure that he would.

Colin had seemed inordinately pleased to go. She thought it was because he was annoyed at her for saying how much she was looking forward to a night out with Will, and she didn't like his smirk when he left, saying, 'Have a good time tonight, now.' But she didn't give him the satisfaction of knowing he had bothered her. She just smiled and said,

'I'm sure I will.'

He hadn't returned by the time they left, though, and Anna was getting worried. 'He's overdoing it,' she complained to Will. 'He's only been home five days.'

'Salty'll watch him. Don't worry. That's what tonight's for—to get away from our responsibility.'

Anna wished it was as easy as that. But as they wound through tree-covered hills, then turned off the highway on to a gravel road that dipped and curved through a canopy of birches and maples until it finally opened on to a clearing where several cars were already parked, she found her mood lightening.

'It's lovely,' she exclaimed, delighted with the newly mown field dotted with spreading oak trees. 'There's even a stream!' She bounded out of the car the moment it stopped, then helped Will unload the salads they had brought.

'You get the blanket,' he directed. 'I'll carry these.' And he led her down the path to where three tables had been strategically placed in the shade of the largest oak. Several women were already there setting out what appeared to be several hundred pounds of delicious food.

'Good grief,' Anna said involuntarily, stunned at the sight of all the bounty and hoping their salads measured up to these. 'Are you expecting an army?'

Will shook his head. 'All good Wisconsin picnics are like this.'

'I'm surprised you are not all overweight then,' Anna retorted, looking over his lean frame with new respect.

'We work it off, he grinned. 'Come on, I'll introduce you.'

Her performed half a dozen introductions so quickly that Anna only saw a blur of faces bedecked with smiles. Only a middle-aged physics professor who had gone to UCLA stood out in her mind. When he seemed inclined to stop and chat she was grateful. More new faces she did not need. Still, she found herself only half-listening to his monologue on California beaches, instead finding herself wondering what Colin was doing, if he'd got home, and even (horrors!) wishing he were with them. Immediately she was annoyed that she had wished it. She tried to pay closer attention to the monologue, but she feared she had looked too glassy-eyed to redeem herself and, as he wandered off, she promised herself she would do better on the next person she met. She was vastly relieved when Will reappeared to press a cold beer into her hands and say, 'I have some more people I want you to meet.'

She turned, smiling, as he introduced, 'This is Mike Tate, our director of Student Services, and his wife, Cindy.'

'Pleased to meet you,' Mike Tate said in one of those deep, sexy voices that Anna associated with movie stars. He took her hand in his and she felt she ought to curtsey or something. He was classically handsome, more so even than Rich, with blond, straight hair swept back off his forehead, and ocean blue eyes that set off a deep tan that spoke more of Hawaii or California than Wisconsin. His wife Cindy was more of the same. She was a gorgeous blonde, the kind who definitely have more fun, about twenty-five, with a pretty, fine boned face. They should have been models, Anna thought. They were wasted here.

Anna shook Cindy's hand too, mumbling something about being glad to meet her, when she noticed Cindy's quizzical expression and saw that the other woman was looking hard at her left hand. For a moment Anna was puzzled, but then realised that Cindy must be wondering about it and what she was doing with William. She was probably concerned about what had happened to Andrea, whom he was supposed to be engaged to, but was too polite to ask.

'This is Anna Douglas, from California,' Will was saying. 'She's living with us and is going to be teaching sixth grade in the fall.'

'Oh?' Cindy was obviously still intrigued. Then she said brightly, obviously having figured out how to broach the subject. 'Are you engaged?'

'Yes, but . . .' Anna began.

'But not to Will,' came a decidedly familiar voice, and Colin's arm dropped over her shoulder as though it belonged there, and he pulled her against him.

'Colin!' Cindy looked as astonished as Anna felt. Anna herself just stared, open-mouthed, up into his face. And he took it as provocation apparently, for he bent his head and brushed his lips lightly across her cheek, stopping at her still open mouth, kissing her with a thoroughness that went far beyond his first kiss. Her amazement gave way to rage.

'Colin! What . . .' she struggled to push herself away from him, but his grip was like iron and he wasn't giving her an inch. Even in his weakened state he was still far too strong to push around.

'Surprised you, didn't I?' he grinned. 'She and Will were going to let me take it easy tonight,' he explained to Mike and Cindy. 'I've been recuperating from malaria. But,' he gave Anna another quick squeeze, 'I decided I couldn't let her out of my sight.'

'Colin!' Anna protested, stepping hard on his foot.

'You don't have to be embarrassed,' he said to her in that maddeningly calm, indulgent tone that infuriated her. 'Cindy and Mike haven't been married long. They understand how I feel, don't you?' he asked them.

'Sure,' Mike grinned, all questions answered. He seemed delighted at Colin's news, but Cindy made a strangled sound that Anna found hard to interpret.

'Well,' Will broke in, 'you could've just said you wanted her to stay home with you. I'd never want to come between lovebirds.'

Not him too! Why on earth was Will playing along

with this nonsense? Anna glared at him, but he smiled equably, apparently willing to go along with Colin's ridiculous deception and obviously expecting her to do so as well.

Seeing no way out short of calling Colin a liar, which she was tempted to do but for the knowledge that he could break her in half, she asked Cindy, 'Did you just get married then?'

'At Easter,' Cindy replied. Then she turned to Colin and said sweetly, 'Pity you were out in the jungle and couldn't make it to the wedding.'

'Yes. But I'll be having one of my own before long, won't I, Anna?' He looked at her with a wicked glint in his eye.

Two could play that game, Anna decided. So she slipped her arm around his waist and dug her fingers into his ribs. 'If you say so, Colin,' she simpered.

He caught her hand, squeezing it hard. 'Well see you again, I'm sure,' he said to Mike and Cindy as if dismissing them. 'I'll be around for a while now.' He gazed down at Anna as though she were the reason, and she felt her cheeks go crimson. Damn him anyway! She hoped he couldn't feel her heart beating like a wildcat inside her chest. He would really laugh if he had any idea how much he was affecting her.

Mike winked. 'See you around then,' he said, and Cindy had apparently recovered from whatever was strangling her enough to blind them with her smile, but Anna noticed that her eyes were hard as ice. They moved away to talk to some other friends, and Colin's grip gradually eased. As soon as the Tates were out of earshot Anna whirled to face him, spluttering, 'Whatever do you mean by . . .'

'Not here,' he said through his teeth.

'I'll just go and fetch us some food,' Will said quickly. 'Go sit on the blanket under the tree. I'll be right back.' He started towards the tables and then thought better of it. 'You come too,' he said to Anna, grabbing her arm. He must have sensed that leaving her with Colin was not a judicious idea.

'Do you know what he's doing?' she hissed at William as he dragged her to the buffet line.

'I think so.'

'Well, what?'

'Let him explain later.'

'I am not engaged to him!'

'*I* know that.'

'Well, Cindy and Mike Tate certainly don't!'

'I think that was the general idea,' Will said drily. 'Don't worry about it. No one will make you marry him. Here,' he thrust a plate at her. 'Take plenty. We don't want to have to go through this line twice. And get enough for Colin.'

'Don't trust me,' Anna cautioned. 'I might put arsenic in.'

Will laughed. 'It's not that bad.'

'How could anyone think I was engaged to that—to that—'

'He's not bad looking,' Will said smiling.

'We're not talking about looks. He's a snake ... A rat ... A ...'

'Shh. You're talking about your betrothed.' He laughed again at the glare she gave him. 'Careful you don't drop your fork.' He led the way back to the blanket where Colin was stretched out, squinting up at an older lady who looked like Mrs Santa Claus. When Anna walked up to them the lady turned and asked, 'Is this the young lady, Colin? She's lovely.'

'Thank you,' he said lazily. 'Yes, this is Anna, Mrs Pullen.'

Anna's eyes widened. How many people was he going to tell, for heaven's sake? 'Hello,' she said rather woodenly.

'Hello, my dear. I just heard from Cindy Tate that you're going to marry this scamp. I must say it was quite a surprise.'

'Yes,' Anna agreed. It was. She glared murderously at Colin.

'Well, congratulations to you both,' Mrs Pullen said, bestowing another beaming smile on them before she moved away.

'News travels fast,' Colin murmured, a smile quirking the corner of his mouth.

'Sit up and take this plate before I dump these baked beans down your neck,' Anna snapped. 'How could you do that? Where did you come from? How did you get here?'

Colin hauled himself to a sitting position and leaned back against the tree, balancing the plate on his knees. 'Thanks. It's good,' he said with his mouth full. 'To answer your questions: One, it seemed like a good idea at the time; two, I was up at Salty's place; and three, I walked down. It's only about a quarter of a mile.'

'Congratulations,' someone called to them, and Colin grinned and waved. 'Smile,' he directed Anna. 'Look happy.'

'You're insane,' she hissed through a Cheshire-cat smile. 'You should be home in bed. I think your afternoon out has affected your brain.'

'Maybe,' he conceded. 'I am tired.' He finished shovelling the food off his plate in silence and then wiped his mouth. Twisting around and lying back, he rested his head in her lap. 'Mmmmm. Nice.'

Anna bolted to her feet, dropping his head on to the ground with a thump. 'I am not your pillow! I am not your fiancée! I don't know where you get off thinking you can . . .'

'Excuse us,' Colin said to Will who was staring at them with interest. 'We'll be right back.' He sprang lithely to his feet and, grasping Anna's arm, hauled her down towards the stream in the opposite direction from the picnicking crowd.

'Let me go!' She writhed and twisted, but Colin's grip was like steel, and she gave up after a poorly aimed kick at his shin only caused him to reach down and swing her up into his arms, scarcely even breaking his stride.

'If I collapse after this, it'll be your fault,' he muttered as he staggered down to the stream and dumped her ignominiously on the bank.

'You great oaf! My fault? Who started this?' She

glared up at him, eyes spitting fire, and Colin dropped heavily to the ground beside her.

'You did,' he insisted. 'If you hadn't been living at Will's . . .'

'Oh, don't start that again. My God, the number of things you blame on me living at the Fieldings' when you didn't approve is as many as the human race can blame on Adam and Eve. Pretty soon it'll have the status of original sin! Now, I repeat, why did you say we were engaged?'

He looked uncomfortable, as though he had hoped he would not have to answer that. 'That woman you met,' he said finally, twisting a root which was growing out of the bank. 'Cindy Tate . . .'

'I know her name. What about her?' She had seemed nothing more than a two-dimensional paper doll type to Anna, though admittedly she was nice to look at.

'She's the one I was engaged to.'

'Cindy Tate?' It was impossible to keep the incredulous tone out of her voice entirely, and Colin heard it and shot her a wry look.

'I've grown up since,' he said roughly.

I should hope so, was on the tip of her tongue, but she recognised how catty it would sound even before she didn't say it, and contented herself with observing, 'She's an attractive woman.'

'Yes.' His voice was clipped. Hiding an edge of irritation? she wondered. Had Cindy thrown him over to date and then marry Mike Tate? He had never told her the circumstances of his broken engagement, only had sounded bitter that it had happened. The fires of Anna's curiosity raged, but one look at Colin's closed face and she knew she wasn't going to get any satisfaction there. He had strangled the root and was working on destroying a large rock now.

Anna said, 'Is that why you wanted her to think I was engaged to you? Because of your own broken engagement?'

'Something like that.' He dug at the rock with an intensity that might have meant that he was paying only marginal attention to their conversation, but Anna suspected that the opposite was true. For some reason he cared too much. Did he still love Cindy? Was he trying to show her that he wasn't going to sit around pining away after she had married someone else?

'But what good is it going to do? She'll find out we're not.' The implications of what he had done appalled her. What if Rich found out? Not that he was likely to, of course, but it did make everything more difficult. He was so sensible and moderate in his behaviour that he would never get himself in a messy business like this. She doubted if he would be able to understand how she had. She wasn't sure she understood it herself. Since Toby she had gone out of her way to avoid anything remotely resembling a demanding or complex relationship or situation. She had refused to commit herself to anything or anyone more demanding than Rich.

Until now. And since she had walked into Colin Davies's life she had felt like she was drowning.

'Why does she have to find out?' he was asking. He didn't look at her, studying his rock excavations with the intensity of a landscape architect.

'Because I'm not engaged to you. I am engaged to Rich Howell, and I am going to marry him at the end of the school year. It should be very obvious then to everyone that I'm not engaged to you!' She felt as though she were trying to explain the theory of relativity to a six year old, getting nowhere fast. Colin looked like it was she who was crazy, not him.

'I thought I proved to you that you didn't love him?' he sighed.

'You did no such thing! Anyway, you apologised afterwards. And you ought to be apologising again right now. If you think I'm going to stay here and listen to you go on about things you know nothing about and . . .'

'All right, all right,' he put in quickly. 'I apologise again. For that time, for this time, for whatever you want. Let's not get into trivial arguments when . . .'

'My engagement is not trivial!'

'No, it's not,' he agreed solemnly. 'That's why I want to use it.' He ran his hand through already ruffled hair. 'I need to be engaged.' He looked driven into a corner, and Anna suddenly felt a pang of pity for him. And a stab of jealousy. Cindy Tate must have a great deal more to her than just stunning looks if Colin felt this badly about losing her and wanted to go to such extraordinary lengths just to put on a good show before her and her new husband.

'For how long?' she asked tentatively.

He grinned at her. 'I knew you would,' he said, looking suddenly better. 'Oh, I don't know how long. Long enough to give them all something to talk about. Besides,' he added, 'you might get to like it!'

Anna knew she might. Too much. She'd had the devil's own time trying to keep Colin in the background of her life ever since she'd been here. She must be crazy to agree to let him go on pretending they were engaged. How would she ever keep him from invading her mind at every moment then?

I only wanted a little temptation, she thought ruefully, and remembered her father once saying, 'Be careful what you pray for. You just might get it!'

Amen, Anna thought, docilely allowing Colin to loop his arm around her shoulders and lead her back to the picnic. Amen.

CHAPTER FIVE

WHILE Anna expected to find by the next afternoon that her 'engagement' to Colin was common knowledge among the faculty and anyone else interested in the whole of Belle River, she had not expected Colin to 'go public' with it. So she was taken aback when she returned from the library where she had been doing some work for William to find him lolling by the front door as though waiting for her, and even more surprised when he said, 'How about celebrating our engagement with dinner?'

'What?' She had just endured three hours of whisperings-behind-the-back and speculative glances galore, all, she was certain, to do with her supposed engagement to Colin Davies, and she was having strong second thoughts about the whole thing. To be invited out to celebrate the cause of her misgivings was a low blow indeed. Especially as Colin was smiling in a way that turned her limbs as well as her resolve to jelly.

'I know a great place,' he went on. 'Besides you need a break. One that you don't have to make potato salad for. Please?' He gave her such a pleading look that it surprised her. She wasn't accustomed to Colin Davies asking for anything. It was impossible to resist.

He knows it, too, she thought when she finally acquiesced. He looked immensely pleased with himself, and she had to remind herself what a good thing it was that she was really engaged to Rich. Colin Davies could tear her heart to shreds if she would let him.

Having got used to Colin in what she had come to think of as his 'uniform', that is, cut-offs and nothing else, she felt a small tremor of shock when she saw him waiting for her that evening in the parlour. He wore a very well-tailored light blue suit, a pristine white shirt, and a regimental striped tie. He got to his feet

76

immediately and held out his hand to give her the lacy white shawl she had left on the couch. 'You look lovely,' he said.

'You do too,' she replied honestly, and then blushed.

Colin laughed. 'First time my date ever told me that.'

Confused, Anna took refuge in their charade. 'Well, I'm not your date really. I'm your pseudo-fiancée.'

'Yes,' he agreed gravely. 'You are.' Their eyes caught. Anna felt a treacherous little voice inside her clearing its throat. 'I wish it were real,' the voice said, before she could squelch the though, and nervously she looked away, afraid that he could read her mind.

But he only said, 'I've got reservations for eight. Let's go for a drive first.'

'Are you sure?' Anna asked. He still had to be careful about overdoing things. And in more ways than one, Anna thought, this evening with Colin might be overdoing things. But he shook his head, not pleading now, but implacable.

'I'm fine,' he said firmly. 'And if I collapse later, you can drive home.' He took her arm and led her out the door without allowing further protest, helping her into his battered Datsun, and heading south on the highway out of town. He didn't say anything, content apparently to enjoy the scenery, and Anna took her cue from him. She didn't think she was going to be able to make small talk for long anyway. The way they looked at each other seemed to preclude it. But the silence wasn't an uncomfortable one. She found it companionable, and when he stopped once to show her where he had hunted arrowheads as a boy, she was enchanted with the idea of Colin as a child and with the thought of coming back someday and looking for arrowheads herself.

'We can, if you want,' he said offhandedly. 'Are you sure?'

'Of course I'm sure. I'd love to.'

'Most women wouldn't.' It was a flat statement with no room for discussion.

Possibly not, Anna conceded silently, but how many had he asked? Unless he just meant Cindy. That was possible. 'Well, I'm not most women,' she said. 'When would you be well enough?'

'Oh, in a week or so, don't you think?'

'I'll make sure you are,' she laughed. 'Otherwise I won't get to come.'

'Yes, you'll have to take good care of me or you won't get your treat,' he teased, laughing at her. But it didn't raise her ire this time, and she grinned back at him, letting him take her arm as they walked back to the car through a grassy field, feeling a faint flickering of hope or happiness that she hadn't felt before.

Colin must have felt it, too, for when he opened the door for her even his eyes were smiling, and he bent to touch her lips with his very gently, as if—were he to unleash any passion—it might spoil the tenderness of the moment. Anna sank into the seat of the car, dazed and thoughtful, as though she'd had several glasses of wine on an empty stomach, entirely unable to think straight, aware only of the strong male body that slid into the cramped space next to her. She had an almost overwhelming desire to inch over next to him so that his muscular thigh pressed against hers.

Colin had made reservations at one of Belle River's better restaurants. Anna had heard plenty of talk about it, but she'd never been there, and she was pleased to discover that it was everything people claimed. The decor was warm and inviting, the service impeccable, and the food delicious—at least as far as she noticed. Her attention was almost entirely focused on Colin. The flame of happiness that had been kindled earlier grew stronger and more overpowering as the evening wore on. It was hard to remember that they were 'acting', it all seemed so right. They laughed and talked and argued amicably over a whole field of topics, and Anna looked at him, smiling across the candles and wine glasses, and thought quite suddenly, I've never been so happy. But she couldn't stop and reflect on it because just then Colin said something so utterly absurd that she broke up laughing, and didn't stop until he admonished,

'No more wine for you! One of us has to drive home. And it isn't going to be me.'

'Are you feeling sick?' she asked quickly, sobering up and looking at him with real alarm.

'No. But I have no intention of pushing my luck. Especially not when you're all healthy and ready to take over. Besides,' he stood up and held out his hand, 'I want to spend the rest of my strength doing something far more pleasant. Dance?'

Surprised, but pleased, Anna got to her feet, feeling not unlike Cinderella at the ball. It had been that sort of night—everything larger than life, all perceptions heightened. You're besotted, she told herself frankly as he led her on to the dance floor. But the glow of wine and well-being didn't diminish, and she slipped into his arms with the sense of finally having come home. Almost unconsciously she slid her arms up around his neck, toying with the dark hair that brushed his collar.

'Mmmmm,' he murmured, resting his cheek against her hair, his arms locking behind her to mould her body to his. They were scarcely dancing at all, just swaying in time to the music, the heat between them growing until Anna thought they might burst into flame. It was a thousand times more seductive than what she'd learned at dancing school. Mrs Pottebaum, her teacher, would have been shocked. Anna, four hours ago, would have been shocked too. But now she was beyond shock, beyond sense, wanting only for Colin to go on holding her, for the feeling growing between them to find satisfaction, for the music never to end.

'Well, look who's here,' she heard a sultry voice beside her, and her shoulder was jostled. Splinters of reality pierced her two-person world.

'Hello,' Colin said, his grip on Anna tensing before it slackened. Anna lifted her face away from his shoulder to see the well-coiffured blonde head of Cindy Tate just as the music died away.

'Have you eaten?' Cindy asked, snuggling against Mike while she batted big blue eyes at Colin.

'Yes. We were just about to leave.' Colin moved

towards the edge of the dance floor, keeping Anna firmly against him.

'Have a drink with us before you go,' Cindy cooed. 'For old time's sake.' Anna thought her wheedling tone was the closest thing to fingernails on a blackboard that she'd heard and that leaving was a grand idea, but Colin said,

'Maybe a quick one,' and dug his fingers into Anna's elbow with enough force to make her 'All right' come out more like a squeak than an acceptance.

The Tates had been seated on the other side of the dining room from their own table and had apparently just arrived and were waiting for their own dinner, dancing until it was served. Abysmal luck them showing up here, Anna thought, but Colin didn't seem to think so. He was chatting easily with Mike, ignoring Cindy who looked increasingly annoyed but who didn't seem to deem a conversation with Anna worth having. All of Anna's small talk failed her when Cindy met it with monosyllables, gaze nailed on Colin's rugged face, and Anna thought irritably, if you're so enthralled, dearie, why didn't you marry *him*? Because there were no two ways about it: Cindy was practically sitting there with her tongue hanging out. Anna would have liked to have throttled her. Her own husband was every bit as good looking and clearly in love with her. But tonight at least she seemed only to have eyes for Colin Davies.

'We really should be going,' Anna said after they had finished their drinks. 'Colin's not supposed to over-exert himself.'

'Oh, but he looks wonderful,' Cindy protested. 'And, listen, Colin, they're playing that song! I never could remember the name of it, but remember when . . .'

'I remember,' Colin said abruptly, supplying the name, and starting to get to his feet.

'Then you'll just have to dance with me to it,' Cindy simpered. She slipped out from beneath Mike's arm and gave Colin one of her best come-on smiles. 'Dance with Annie, Mike,' she told her husband, who looked as discomfited as Anna, but who obediently rose to his feet and escorted her to the dance floor.

'You needn't,' Anna protested as he swept her away, but Mike said,

'I'd enjoy it.'

He was a better actor than she was, Anna thought. Or else he really didn't care that his wife was practically assaulting another man in a public place. He certainly didn't give a clue to what he was thinking, and Anna wished she could emulate him. As it was she could hardly keep from craning her neck to see Cindy and Colin. And she ground her teeth in fury when she spotted them swaying in a dark corner, Cindy's aqua sheath dress glued to Colin's muscular form.

If the music had seemed too short when she was dancing with Colin herself, it stretched on infinitely now. The dance floor wasn't crowded so Anna was usually afforded a clear view of Cindy cuddling up to Colin, and if she had felt warm from his embrace earlier, it was nothing to the way she was boiling with anger now. She didn't know who she was angrier at— Cindy who was making it happen, or Colin who was letting her. For someone who was supposedly trying to show his ex-fiancée how in love he was with his present one, he was certainly not holding Cindy at arm's length. If she got any closer, Anna thought grimly, you'd think they were Siamese twins. Once he caught Anna's eye and gave her a mocking grin, as though he were trying to use Cindy to make her jealous rather than using Anna to prove to Cindy that he didn't care about her anymore. Anna glared back at him, and stepped on Mike's toes so engrossed was she in hating Colin for bending his head to hear Cindy's whispers and then laughing.

'Sorry,' she mùmbled to Mike. 'I'm very clumsy tonight. Perhaps we should sit down.' Mike managed to smile through what started as a painful grimace, but he showed no hesitation about leading her back to their table.

'Another glass of wine?' he offered.

'No thank you.' Making her excuses, she left him at the table and went to the restroom where she repinned her hair, noting with mortification that Colin had almost completely unpinned it, so that it hung about her shoulders loosely. While she was pinning it she gave herself a firm lecture about not letting her emotions get involved and wished that they would get home before she started playing the jealous fiancée for real. Why wasn't Colin acting cool and distant with Cindy? Why play with fire?

A good question. One you ought to ask yourself, Anna Douglas, she chastised herself. Even pretending to be engaged to Colin Davies was playing with fire. And she was in grave danger of being burned.

By the time she got back to the table Cindy and Colin had returned. Anna took advantage of the fact that Colin was still on his feet to put an entreating hand on his arm and give him the sort of winning smile that, had it not been backed by gritted teeth, would have melted many a masculine heart. Colin's, it seemed, wasn't affected, the twinkle in his eye attested to that, but he nodded when she said, 'I think we should be going now,' and helped her slip on her shawl.

'Good to see you,' he said to the Tates. 'I'd like to talk to you again about some of those in-the-field seminars, Mike. Maybe we can work something out.'

'Let's try,' the other man said, and Cindy purred,

'We'll invite you for dinner soon. Bye-bye, Annie.'

A grin slashed Colin's face. 'Yeah, we'll have to do that.' He took Anna's arm, 'Come along, Annie. Time we went home.'

'However do you expect to give her the impression that you don't care for her when you let her drape herself all over you like some sort of fur coat?' Anna demanded, rounding on him once they were outside in the still, warm night.

'Was that what she was doing?' Colin was still grinning, his hand lightly caressing her waist, and she stepped forward quickly in an effort to shake him off, but he wouldn't be shaken.

'You know damned well it was! Lord, she just hung there!'

'Jealous?' he teased. 'Imagine being jealous of a mink coat.'

'Not mink. Weasel more likely. And I was not jealous.'

'You gave a very good impression of it.'

'I'm a very good actress,' she lied, not willing to acknowledge her actual rage. The implications were too messy. If she was truly jealous of Cindy, why *was* she engaged to Rich?

'Very,' Colin agreed. His grip tightened and he swung her around, capturing her in his arms, kissing her long and hard. 'God,' he muttered, fingers tangling in her hair, unpinning it again. 'I've been wanting to do that for hours. Kiss me, Anna.' His lips came down again, and her mouth opened under his probing, reluctance vanishing in his assault on her senses. She kissed him, wanting him as much as he wanted her, seeking to know, to confirm, all the feelings they had shared, all the warm, heady, drugging feelings that sapped her reason, destroyed her common sense, and left her reeling, aching, longing. It was Colin who pulled away first, his breathing ragged, unsteady, his head bent, resting on her shoulder, his hands gripping her upper arms so tightly that she knew he would leave bruises.

'Was that acting?' His voice was a bare whisper, and Anna closed her eyes, too shaken to answer. Her fists clenched and unclenched as she struggled for composure. She could not have meant it! She would not allow herself to have meant it! Feelings like that for Colin Davies were as destined to be unrequited as her feelings for Toby had once been. He was only trying to prove to her that she didn't love Rich—just as he'd done once before. It didn't mean that, other than a natural male desire, Colin Davies felt a thing for her.

'I told you I was good, didn't I?' she said, trying for an even tone that wouldn't betray the unsteadiness of her emotions. It apparently convinced him, for he lifted his head and gave her a long, hard look. Curious? Pained? She couldn't be sure, and shrugged slightly as he said,

'You drive, huh? I'm bushed.'

Neither one of them said another word all the way home.

The next day he could barely drag himself out of bed.

'My head hurts,' he complained, grimacing when she bustled in and pulled up the blinds.

'Hangover?'

He groaned. 'Hardly. But Whitmeyer did say not to drink anything ...'

'Why didn't you tell me?' she whirled on him, glaring, taking in the greyish cast to his skin, the sunken eyes and lined forehead.

'I didn't think a bit of wine would make any difference.' He put a hand over his eyes to shut out the light. 'Obviously I was wrong.'

He did look awful, and she felt immediately contrite for her earlier flippancy. But she hadn't slept well herself, and had considered his own late rising to just be more of the same.

'Can I get you anything?' she asked now, going over to him, barely able to resist the urge to stroke his dishevelled hair and rough cheek.

All her tossings and turnings were forgotten in the face of his misery, and when he muttered, 'How about a bucket?' she didn't feel the slightest compulsion to smile.

'That bad?'

'Mmmmmm,' he murmured, eyes still hidden by the arm flung over his face. 'I don't dare sit up.'

So she sat down on the edge of the bed and reached for his hand, and he lifted his arm and looked at her. She was instantly reminded of his look of the previous evening in the aftermath of their kiss, and she could feel the heat growing in her cheeks, but she forced herself to meet his gaze. It was not that she loved him, she told herself, it was just that he was another human being, ill and in need of comfort, and she couldn't turn away. He gave her a wan smile, his fingers pressing into the palm of her hand, and he closed his eyes. I don't love him, she thought wildly. I can't!

But it became harder and harder to keep telling herself that. He bounced back quickly from his relapse after their night out, and while he was careful not to overdo it again, he still found the time and energy to go for walks in the evening with her, to meet her at the student union for coffee when she took a break from her work for William, and to behave generally in the way that a loving fiancé should behave in public. In private, too, she had to admit. His hands never dropped to his sides when they came indoors, instead he reached for her— caressing, stroking, tormenting, until she thought she would go mad. Whether from longing or from apprehension she was never quite sure. In either case, she was in a constant state of turmoil, experiencing mental urges which told her to stop this pseudo-engagement and all the dallying that went with it at once, and physical urges, emotional urges, which refused to let her.

'The week is up,' Colin announced one afternoon when he met her at the union, 'and I'm ready.'

Anna looked at him puzzled.

'We're going arrowhead hunting today.'

It had been one of those mornings when she had got absolutely nothing done for Will that she hadn't had to do over three times. Her mind had been on other things (brown hair, deep brown eyes, long tapered fingers on calloused hands, a hair roughened chest above cut-off jeans), and she had almost convinced herself that she could take no more, that she would have to tell him that their fake engagement was off. But her resolve vanished in the face of a beguiling grin and the promise of an arrowhead hunt.

'Really?' She gulped her coffee, scalding her tongue. 'Marvellous. Are you sure it's okay? You won't have another relapse?'

'I'm sure. You're an excellent nurse. And if you smile at me like that I'd go with you whether I was dying or not!'

She knew he didn't mean it, but it didn't take the joy out of the day. She was out of the union and walking briskly towards home to change her clothes before Colin could catch up with her.

For the rest of the day he watched her with an expression which varied between incredulity, amazement and indulgent amusement. He didn't believe at first that she was really as interested as she had sounded. And then when they actually got to the field where he told her she might find some arrowheads, he seemed to expect her to give up immediately or to expect him to do all the looking. When she didn't, instead telling him to sit down and take it easy while she sloughed back and forth, up and down the rows of an unplanted field, eyes to the ground searching for bits of points and shatter, he stared at her, astonished.

'Truly,' she said, giving him a shove towards the edge of the field. 'You've shown me more or less what to look for. You don't have to keep walking with me. Rest, for heaven's sake. You're the authority. You just sit there and tell me what I've found.'

What he told her she found during the rest of the afternoon was two bits of seashells, the back molar of a pig, a rusty tractor bolt, one broken point and several small pieces of shatter.

'Not bad,' he consoled her. 'For a beginner.'

'Not bad?' she sniffed. 'I thought it was marvellous! I mean, three hours ago I wouldn't even have known that these jagged, sharp bits of stone were anything to do with early Indians. I'd have thought they were crumbled bits of rock or something.' She gave him a sweaty, grimy grin, and wiped a dirt encrusted hand across her face. 'That was really neat.'

Colin laughed. 'You're certainly easy to please.' He allowed her to haul him to his feet and slinging an arm over her shoulder he led her back to the car. 'Now I'll take you to dinner. To celebrate your discoveries!'

Anna looked shocked. 'Like this? Colin, I'm filthy. I can't go out to dinner!'

'Nonsense. Where I'm taking you, you'll fit right in.'

Unless it was a pigpen, Anna doubted that. But he had that implacable look on his face again, the one that dared her to argue with him, and they had had such a lovely day that she didn't want to spoil it now, so she kept silent and prayed that what he had in mind was the Dairy Queen.

It wasn't. He stopped about a mile further up the road, turning on to a gravel drive which dipped precariously down a hillside into some woods before splashing through a small creek.

'A very out of the way restaurant,' Anna said mystified.

'Salty's,' Colin explained, pulling up into the dusty front yard of an aging but well-kept farm house. Two spaniels bounded off the porch to greet him, wagging tails that bespoke friendly relations, and Salty came round the corner of the barn and gave them a wave.

'We've come for dinner,' Colin hollered, getting out of the car. 'You remember Anna?'

'Of course.' Salty grinned at her, apparently amused but not put off by her filthy appearance. 'What are you fixing us to eat?' he asked Colin.

'I'll check the cupboards,' Colin said and started for the house. 'Come on, you can scrub up in here,' he told Anna, who followed him obediently, amazed at the nonchalance with which Salty accepted Colin barging in and at Colin's assumption that it was his right to do so. Colin showed her the bathroom, took an appraising glance at her dirty jeans and shirt and reappeared a moment later with a clean pair of jeans and a man's shirt.

'Try these,' he said. 'They'll be a bit big, but I suspect they'll be an improvement over what you've got on.'

'I can't wear Salty's things,' Anna protested, though she would have dearly loved a change.

'They're mine,' Colin told her. 'I keep stuff here. Sometimes I live here for months.'

She wanted to say that she couldn't wear his clothes either, that it put them on entirely too intimate a footing for her peace of mind, but he tossed the clothes on to the clothes hamper and went back to the kitchen before she could open her mouth. Shrugging, she squashed her compunctions and stripped off her field-working clothes, scrubbing off vigorously with a wash cloth that Colin had provided, and dressing again in his jeans and shirt. Being tall herself, she didn't have to roll up the legs very much, and though the shirt was baggy, with the sleeves rolled up it didn't fit too badly. All she really needed was a belt. Holding the jeans up she padded barefoot back to the kitchen and told Colin.

He was hunkered down, sorting through the cans in Salty's cupboards, trying to decide on their meal apparently, and when she emerged he looked over his shoulder at her, then stood up and grinned. 'Not bad. I like it without the belt. Adds a certain sense of adventure and daring.'

'Ha, ha,' Anna said. 'Surely Salty must have an extra one.'

'I wouldn't know,' Colin replied, his hands busy unbuckling his. 'You can wear mine.' He slipped it off and went over to her, shrugging off her outstretched hand, and threading it through the loops in her jeans himself. He was so close he was literally breathing down her neck, and Anna felt goose bumps prickling up and down her spine.

'I can do it,' she said hastily, trying to edge away from him. But he held her fast, one hand moving the belt, the other tracing seductive patterns against her back and ribs. 'Stop that! I'm ticklish!' She wriggled away for a moment, but he caught her again, pinning her between the refrigerator and his hard chest, feathering kisses on her cheeks, across the bridge of her nose, finally teasing her lips.

'Better?' he murmured.

It didn't tickle now, if that was what he meant. But it made her weak-kneed and dizzy, and, under the circumstances, she wasn't sure it was an improvement at all. 'Stop it,' she ordered, pushing against his chest. 'Colin! Behave!'

'I am,' he retorted, his hips still pressing intimately against her. 'I am behaving like a normal, red-blooded fiancé ought to behave!'

'You are not my fiancé!' Despite all her traitorous feelings, she was still engaged to Rich, and no one knew it better than Colin. Why did he persist in tempting her this way? 'Just give me the belt and leave me alone.'

He didn't answer. The door opened at that moment and Salty came in. He took a long look at Anna's flushed face and ruffled hair and remarked, 'Bit slow with dinner, aren't you, Colin?'

'Distractions,' Colin mumbled. But he turned back to the cupboard, banging cans and pots and pans, and Salty grinned at Anna who hurriedly finished buckling the belt Colin gave her while nervously grinning back.

'Colin said you were interested in arrowheads,' Salty politely changed the subject. 'Like to see mine?'

'Oh yes.' As much, she thought, to get out of Colin's way as to actually see Salty's collection. She followed him into a room he used as a study and gasped in delight at the rows of arrowheads hung on display boards all around the room. She'd never seen such a collection outside of a museum, and her eager questions kept Salty going until Colin called them to eat.

'If I had known you were this creative,' Anna said through a mouthful of mushroom and cheese omelette, 'I'd have gone to bed and let you cook.'

Colin smiled. 'I'm just proving what a good husband I'll make,' he told her, eyes twinkling, grin broadening at the flush which crept up her cheeks.

'I thought you weren't ever getting engaged again,' she reminded him.

'It's no crime to change your mind.'

Anna's heart quickened. Did he mean it? 'And have you?' she asked. 'Changed your mind?'

Colin shrugged. 'We'll see. I'm trying out pretending to be engaged first,' he teased. 'It depends on how good a job you do as a fiancée.'

'Oh, you . . .' She shook a fist at him.

'Don't pay a bit of attention to him,' Salty said with a fatherly fondness. 'Full of noise, he is. Always was.'

'But a good man in spite of it,' Colin added, grinning. 'But Anna already knows that.' His dark eyes tormented her and she managed to look sceptical without refuting his statement because she sensed that this was a conversation that she might very well drown in. Better to keep silent and just enjoy the bantering between Colin and Salty without getting in the way of it.

Salty, if not Colin, seemed to appreciate her discomfort and steered the conversation into less personal avenues, allowing Anna gradually to relax again and simply enjoy herself. She did, deciding that it was one of the nicest places she'd been in her life. Nothing fancy, everything rather old and utilitarian actually, but Salty's house and furnishings had a hominess and friendliness that warmed her. She leaned back in her chair, replete, and watched Colin argue good-naturedly with Salty over the likelihood of finding pottery remains in some caves near the river, not hearing the words so much as the closeness and comradeship between the two of them. This was a Colin she had never seen before. Even with Will and Jenny he hadn't seemed this relaxed; he had always been sharper, more intense. It was, she thought, an unlucky bit of fate witnessing it. It made him seem more likeable than ever. The spikiness was softened, the rough edges smoothed, all his attractiveness simply heightened in her eyes.

Damn, she thought. Oh damn. She couldn't help feeling sorry when they left. It was a magical day, even if it had left her more vulnerable than ever.

'You're kidding,' Jenny said, visibly astonished when Anna told her the next day where they had been.

'No, why?'

'Not just anybody goes to Salty's.' It sounded like an invitation to the White House. 'I don't think Colin's ever taken anyone else there. And the only person Will has ever taken is Andrea.'

'I think,' Anna replied, laughing, 'that you have to be a certain type of person to appreciate it. The mud-loving, dog-loving, horse-loving sort. Probably there aren't many of those around. At least among Colin's girl friends.' Cindy Tate for instance was not that sort Anna knew without question.

Jenny considered this. 'Maybe. You've certainly got under his guard.'

No more than he's got under mine, Anna thought, but she went on brushing her hair in silence, unable or unwilling to contradict Jenny's claim. Whether Jenny would have pursued her line of thought Anna would never know for at that moment the 'phone rang and Jenny raced to answer it. She was back moments later to announce, 'Guess who.'

It wasn't difficult. Every third or fourth phone call recently had been from Cindy Tate. Apparently her marriage and Colin's engagement didn't deter her when she decided to pursue someone. It was becoming almost a joke around the house.

'You let me think you wanted to be engaged to save face,' Anna had chided Colin the day before when she had waved a fistful of Cindy's 'phone messages in his face. 'And all the while you were really using me for protection.'

A dark flush stained his cheeks and he looked pained. 'Just give me those,' he muttered. 'I'll sort this out . . .' and he had stalked off to his room without looking back.

Now Anna shrugged and said, 'Tell her he won't be back until nine.' He and Will had gone into Dubuque on some errands.

'I did. She wants to talk to you.'

'Me?' Feelings of unease swept over her, but she swallowed hard and took the phone from Jenny. She steeled herself to listen to Cindy gush and was amazed to hear her say simply,

'Tell Colin I've got the tickets for all of us to go to *Othello* on Sunday. We'll pick you up.'

'*Othello*?'

'The Shakespeare Festival, Annie. Didn't he tell you? We discussed it over lunch on Tuesday.' Her words had a breathless quality, as though they were spun instead of spoken.

'Oh yes, of course,' Anna lied. 'It slipped my mind. I'll tell him.' She hung up before Cindy could say anything else. Whatever she might say, Anna was sure she didn't want to hear it. What was all this about *Othello* anyway? Seeing it was a lovely idea. Seeing it with the Tates was a terrible one. She couldn't imagine Colin arranging such a thing. But, she shrugged, if he had, he must have some reason for it. Maybe this was what he meant by 'sorting this out'. Perhaps if they all went out together Cindy would see once and for all that he was not interested, that he was really in love with someone else.

That meant another Academy Award winning performance was going to be required. A whole afternoon of pretending to be Colin's fiancée when she was really Rich's and when she shouldn't care about Colin at all, but did. Her head spun just thinking about it.

She gave Colin Cindy's message about the tickets, and he raised his eyebrows, but then shrugged and said, 'Is it okay with you?' She had talked herself into it by that time so she said yes. But it didn't stop her worrying about it.

She took great pains Sunday to look her best, striving for a casual look with a hint of sophistication because God only knew how far she was from being a big city sophisticate that an LA upbringing might have implied. And she did want to give Cindy something to worry about. There was no use in going if she was going to look so boring and slap-dash that Colin couldn't possibly be interested in her.

Her wardrobe wasn't much to choose from, but she settled on a madras plaid skirt and a gauzy peasant blouse with a scoop neck that called attention to the fullness of her breasts and which generally flattered her slender figure. She could never really compete with Cindy in the figure department, but there was no need to look like a straight edged ruler if she didn't have to. She put her hair up in a loose French twist, even though she knew that Colin would have it down before the day was over, and added a pair of gold hoop earrings that, she concluded, added a modicum of sophistication. Finally she slipped on a pair of strappy sandals with enough heel to allow her to look Colin almost in the eye. He seemed to approve of her efforts for as she went out to the Tates' car with him he slipped an arm around her and murmured, 'Sexy,' in such a low, hungry voice that she turned and pinched him.

'Ouch,' he complained loudly, rubbing his side, and making such a production out of it that Cindy, with barely concealed impatience, snapped,

'Hurry up or we'll miss the dancing,' as though she were chastising a pair of misbehaving adolescents.

It was going to be a long afternoon, Anna decided. And if she had concentrated solely on Cindy it would have been. The other woman spent all her time trying to monopolise Colin's conversation, virtually ignoring her own husband. Anna, mostly to cover for Cindy's bad manners, found herself thrown into conversation with Mike. If Cindy's absorption with Colin bothered him, again he didn't say so. Other than a grim set to his mouth, Mike gave no sign that he was annoyed. He explained about the Renaissance singing and dancing that took place before each performance, telling Anna that sometimes the actors even took part in sword fights or other forms of combat during the pre-performance entertainment. Anna found it enchanting, though she was sure she would have enjoyed it more if she hadn't had to watch Cindy brushing up against Colin every time she moved. Colin didn't seem to be encouraging it. He looked uncomfortable most of the time, tense and strung up, and Anna made it a point to grab his hand just before they went into the theatre.

'You *are* sitting with me, I trust?' she said archly, guessing that if Cindy could have arranged it Anna would have been by herself and Cindy would have been between the two men.

'Of course,' Colin said. And he was. But Cindy was on his other side, whispering to him even more frequently than she whispered to Mike.

Until the lights dimmed and the play began, Anna seethed. But minutes later she had forgotten Cindy Tate, Colin Davies and everything else. She hadn't thought anything could take her mind off the role she was playing that day, but the actor playing Othello gave such life and depth to the character that she forgot her own problems, so caught up was she in his.

She knew, of course, what was coming. She saw the cunning traps set by Iago, and she watched Othello's mistrust grow as he picked up false clues of Desdemona's infidelity. 'Don't you see?' she wanted to shout at him. But of course he didn't. And it was all too possible, she knew, that a person would not. It happened all the time.

'Want to stretch your legs?' Colin asked at intermission. But Anna shook her head, her mind still centuries away.

'We're going out for a bit then,' Cindy announced, taking both mens' arms. 'Mike will get us something to drink.'

'Go ahead.' Anna was content just to sit there and mull, until she was roused by a case of hiccups. They were not an unexpected reaction to emotional upheaval. She got them every once in a while, and she went out to get a drink too. She found Mike standing by the ticket booth alone.

'The lemonade's gone,' he told Anna. 'Cindy and Colin went to get a drink in that building. This machine's on the blink. Maybe you can catch up with them.'

'I'll hurry,' Anna said. She hadn't much intermission left, but she might make it. Dumb of Mike, she thought as she went, letting Cindy and Colin go off together. She was probably pawing him this very instant.

It was Cindy, actually, whom Anna saw first. She had just come abreast of the towering catalpa tree when she stopped dead. There on the steps of the classroom building, almost hidden in the shadows, stood a petite blonde in a flame red pants suit, her arms locked around a tall, dark haired man. Kissing him. Not just any man. Colin.

From somewhere deep inside her, like a spring welling up, came a resounding, 'No!' Anna thought she must have screamed it, but no one moved. She turned and darted behind the tree, flattening herself against it, gasping for air. Then, before she had a chance to move or even think, Colin hurried past the tree alone, heading back towards the theatre. Anna shrank back, afraid of being seen. But he never even glanced up. He was too busy running a hand through mussed hair, no doubt brushing it back into some semblance of order before he had to face Mike again. And her.

'Hello, hello,' Cindy said, seeing Anna crushed against the tree. 'Looking for us?' She gave Anna a saccharine smile and then asked, 'Or did you find us?' It was a double-edged question.

'I found you,' Anna said, even her toes clenching.

'Well, you must understand, dear,' Cindy said calmly. 'Colin and I have known each other for a long, long time. We should have been married but for ... Well, I ...'

'You don't have to explain,' Anna said fiercely, straightening up.

'Just so you understand,' Cindy smiled. 'And don't mind sharing.'

Anna's eyes stared, but Cindy didn't bat a lash. She straightened the jacket to her pants suit and said, 'Everyone seems to be going in now. Shall we?'

'Why not?' Anna grated through clenched teeth, barely able to contain the fury which rose inside her. She didn't need a drink any longer. The hiccups were gone.

CHAPTER SIX

'WHY is it that I get the feeling I've been voted Creep of the Week?' Colin demanded, snatching the paper out of Anna's typewriter and glaring down at her.

'I can't imagine,' she said coolly, taking another sheet and inserting it, beginning to type Will's notes again at the top of the page.

'You can't?' Sarcasm dripped from his words. That paper followed the first into the waste basket, and when she reached for a third, his hand came down hard on top of hers. Eyes duelled until Anna eased her hand slowly out from under his and sighed,

'You seem upset.'

'You're damn right I'm upset!' He stalked over to stare out the window a moment before spinning around, hands on hips, to nail her with another glare. 'I don't understand you.'

You don't understand me? Anna thought a bit hysterically. There's a joke. I suppose you think I understand you. In the week since she had seen Colin and Cindy in their passionate embrace she had tried to think of every possible reason for excusing Colin for it. But it hadn't been easy, especially when she had seen him with Cindy on three different occasions later during the week, and smelled her perfume lingering in his car when he had given Anna a ride to the grocery store, and had answered countless phone calls from a purring female whose identity was only too obvious. If he had wanted to be rid of Cindy, Anna finally realised, he would have been. It was as simple as that.

And since he didn't, she could only suppose he must be using their phoney engagement to cover up an actual illicit relationship with Cindy Tate. It occured to her that if Colin were known to be 'engaged' to a new fiancée of his own, no one would be watching his behaviour with Cindy with nearly the interest that they might give it if he showed up unattached. It was a clever ploy, Anna decided, so clever that she seethed just thinking about it. How dare he tell her he wanted to 'use' her engagement to put off Cindy when in fact he was using it to camouflage his meetings with her!

'What is it you don't understand?' she asked him now, trying for the same cool detachment she had been working on all week. She would have liked to have kicked him—hard—screamed at him, let him know all her hurt at his deception. Only the knowledge that he would have thought it amusing that she even cared, that she might actually let slip her real feelings for him, kept her from doing it.

'Why you're acting like the Ice Queen of the Year.'

'I'm not.'

'Oh, bull! The temperature drops ten degrees when we're in the same room. Not that we're in the same room often. You tend to disappear.'

'You're imagining things.'

'Like hell I am! I come into a room, you leave. I sit down, you stand up. I say, "Hello", you say, "Goodbye". Damn it, what's going on?'

What was going on was her feeble attempt to salvage a bit of her own pride, to ease herself out of his life without a confrontation, without the same weeping anguish she had felt over Toby. And it wasn't working. Not at all.

She might be presenting him with an Ice Maiden façade, but inside she was a raging inferno, bitterly hurt, bitterly angry. But if the truth were known, she wasn't sure if she was angrier at Colin or at herself. She closed her eyes, shutting out his hard, furious face, but it did no good. She had fallen in love with him in spite of everything. Wilfully, stupidly, stubbornly, her heart had defeated her mind. She knew he had no more use for commitments than Toby, she knew he was interested—but not in love, only in going to bed, she knew he was fooling around with Cindy Tate. And damn it, she loved him anyway! She also knew she couldn't let him know it.

'I've just had enough of being your "fiancée",' she said levelly.

'Why?'

'I have a fiancé. Rich Howell.'

Colin rubbed his eyes wearily. 'Don't start that again. You don't love Rich Howell any more than you love William!'

Flags of bright red appeared in Anna's cheeks and she jumped up and shouted, 'You don't know who I love!'

'Do you?' Colin asked coldly, shoving his hands deeply into his jeans pockets and eyeing her harshly.

'Of course,' she said, thinking how true it was even if he didn't believe her. 'You're a fine one to talk. You're making me the laughing-stock of Belle River. You're supposed to be my fiancé, but you spend less time with me than with Cindy Tate!'

A sardonic smile twisted Colin's mouth. 'Jealous, are you?'

'Not on your life!'

'What do you care who I spend time with then? If you're so tired of being my fiancée, of being around me, what difference does it make to you?'

'None,' Anna said quickly, turning to open a file drawer and pretending to search through it. The confrontation wasn't going her way at all.

'I don't believe you,' Colin said, striding over and grasping her by the arms and turning her to face him. 'What's the matter? Afraid that Cindy might be getting a little of what you want?'

'Damn you, of course not!' she twisted to get away from him but his grip was too strong.

'I'll bet you are,' he said, his dark eyes glittering just inches from her own. 'I'll say one thing for Cindy Tate.' A hard smile touched his mouth. 'At least she doesn't promise more than she delivers.'

'You're despicable,' Anna said through her teeth. 'How dare you say a thing like that? I thought you were desperate to avoid Cindy Tate! At least that's what you said. Now you practically live in her pocket.'

Colin shrugged. 'I have my reasons.'

I bet, Anna thought. She kicked him hard in the shin.

'Damn you!' Colin swore, letting her go and hopping around the room rubbing his shin. 'From Ice Maiden to Hellcat in one minute flat!' He swore again softly. 'I'll pay you back for that.'

'You needn't bother,' Anna said, taking refuge behind Will's desk. 'I have quite enough memories of you as is.'

'You need another one,' Colin said, limping towards her.

'No.'

'Oh, yes.' His voice was soft, menacing, and Anna moved back against the file cabinet, kicking over the waste basket. 'You've been asking for this.' His arms pinned on either side of her fastened her to the wall, his dark head bending towards hers.

'I'm not asking for anything,' she stammered.

'Yes, you are. And you've been promising me something too,' he said, his voice thick and hoarse.

'I'm not promising you anything,' Anna said, feeling his hot breath on her cheek, twisting her head in a vain attempt to avoid him. 'The woman you want is Cindy Tate. She's the one with the promises.'

'The hell with Cindy Tate,' Colin muttered, and his mouth swept down to conquer hers, forcing hers to open under the demand of his tongue. At first all she felt was his anger. His frustration crushed her, his strength subdued her weakness. But slowly the kiss changed. His lips, which at the beginning had sought to master, now sought to tease, to cajole. His hands, which had been almost bruising, now stroked and caressed, drawing her against him and tracing erotic patterns on her back and neck, then threaded themselves in the thickness of her hair. Colin groaned, as though he had no control over what was happening, as though he would have stopped if only he could. His heart beat raggedly against hers, and she wanted nothing so much as to give in, to let him go forward and take what she knew she would love to give. But not this way. Not when it meant no more to him than an evening recreation, an assuagement for a temporary itch. Not when she might as easily have been Cindy Tate or God knew how many other attractive young women!

'Stop it,' she begged. 'Stop, Colin!' She was gasping. Her whole being wanted to cry out, 'Yes, go on!' Only knowing that she could not give in when she knew how little it meant to him, kept her sane enough to tell him no.

'Damn it,' he growled, dropping his hands as she twisted away from him. 'Damn it.' He flung himself away and strode to the other side of the room. 'See?' he grated. 'Another promise. No delivery!'

'I didn't promise anything,' she said, her head hanging, hair cascading in disarray around her face.

'Not much,' Colin sneered. 'Is this how you treat Howell? Lead him on and then shut the door?'

'Don't bring Rich into this,' Anna snapped, jerking her head up to glare at him. 'He's worth ten of you.'

A dull red spread across Colin's cheekbones. 'I don't give a damn if he's worth a thousand of me,' he shouted hoarsely. 'You don't love Rich Howell!'

'Go away,' Anna said tonelessly, dropping into her chair and putting her face into her hands. 'Just go away.'

She didn't raise her head again until the clock struck three, long after she had heard his retreating footsteps, the slam of the front door, and the sound of the Datsun scattering gravel as Colin roared away.

He destroyed any semblance of work that she might have pretended to have accomplished that afternoon. She had nothing more than a waste basket full of crumpled papers when she went downstairs at five to cook the bratwurst and sauerkraut that she had bought for supper. She was hoping that a bit of cooking might be therapeutic and that she might think of him with more equanimity after she had puttered around in the kitchen for a while. She did not count on finding him sitting on a stool at the kitchen counter chopping tomatoes.

'What do you think you're doing?' she asked coldly, not looking at him. He had said too much that afternoon for her to know how to look at him anymore. What if he wanted to take up where they had left off?

But Colin seemed to have got selective amnesia for he made no reference to their earlier confrontation, contenting himself with saying, 'I should think that's rather obvious. I'm chopping tomatoes.'

Anna looked at him curiously. 'Why?' They had a schedule for cooking and it was her night, not his.

'I had this overwhelming urge to have tacos,' he explained with a disarming smile. 'Do you mind?'

As he had already chopped the lettuce and grated the cheese, she didn't see where minding would do much good, but she said, 'I suppose not,' in such a grudging tone that he offered,

'I'll cook on my night too, if you want?'

Anna looked at him suspiciously. Colin was not the most willing of cooks at the best of times, though he could do justice to one or two meals. It was hard to accept this conversion to chef, but tacos sounded better than bratwurst on a hot night, and if he was going to do the cooking she could take a walk instead of slaving over the stove. 'Sounds all right to me,' she said cautiously. 'Maybe I'll go out then.'

'Stay and talk to me,' Colin invited, but she shook her head. She had enough trouble dealing with an angry, yelling Colin. To be faced with another one, smiling and congenial just two hours later, was beyond her. What was he playing at? Would she ever figure him out?

'No, thanks. I'll take a stroll. See you at dinner.'

Colin looked rueful. 'Suit yourself,' he said, and she wondered if she detected a note of disappointment in his voice.

She wondered, as she walked, if she would ever be able to detect anything in Colin's voice—or in his behaviour—that would give her a true indication of what he did feel. He was incredibly good, most times, at hiding his emotions. Except the negative ones. It didn't take much to figure out when he was angry. But other times? She shook her head in dismay. At other times he was as elusive as the Sphinx. She didn't even want to think about him, she reminded herself. She had done enough of that all afternoon—to the exclusion of everything else. But despite her wishes to the contrary, her mind stayed in the hot, steamy kitchen where Colin was, though her body strode briskly along the street towards the campus. The warm wind was pleasing on her face, compensating for the sticky humidity still in the air. It was much more tolerable out here than in Will's study where she had been glued to the chair all afternoon. But even the pleasant breeze, the chirping cicadas and the roaring motorcycles didn't succeed in dislodging Colin from her mind. He was a permanent fixture. It was, she thought glumly, as though he had moved in.

Both of him. The fierce, angry, passionate Colin Davies of the afternoon and the smiling, genial one she had just left. How could he switch like that? What was he trying to do?

'Hey, watch it!' a voice sounded in her ear, and she looked up to see Jenny wheeling her bike up to the curb. 'Even in Belle River we have traffic, Anna. Don't dream and cross streets at the same time.'

'Sorry.'

Jenny hopped off her bike and began pushing it alongside Anna. 'Daydreaming about Rich?' she asked. 'Or Colin?' She grinned mischievously. 'How many girls are lucky enough to have two fiancés?'

Anna grimaced. 'It's not all it's cracked up to be,' she said glumly. 'I think I'll ditch one of them. Or maybe both.'

Jenny's eyes widened. 'Really?'

'Just kidding,' Anna said quickly. The last thing she needed was for Jenny to tell Colin that she was thinking of breaking her engagement to Rich. He was insufferably pushy now. If he knew she wasn't engaged, he would be intolerable. And she didn't think her resistance was up to that.

'Oh,' Jenny seemed to be considering this, then shrugged and said, 'Well, if you're planning on dumping one of them, I think Colin would prefer it to be Rich.'

'Colin doesn't want to be engaged to me,' Anna said. He didn't need an engagement to get what he wanted from most girls.

Jenny bit her thumbnail. 'I don't know,' she said slowly. 'I think maybe Colin's in love with you.'

'Don't talk nonsense.'

'I mean it,' Jenny protested. 'He snaps at everyone now. He has all week. When you were always with him he was positively sunny. Now he's more like the God of Thunder. He stomps, he slams, he snarls. I remember when Colin used to be moody sometimes. Now he only has one mood—bad!'

'I don't think that means necessarily that he's in love with *me*,' Anna argued. It could just as easily be that he was finding it hard to sneak around and meet Cindy Tate lately. Or maybe seeing a married woman was giving him a guilty conscience.

'Well, I think it does,' Jenny said obstinately. 'But I don't envy you if he is. Sometimes I think life would be easier without any men in it at all, don't you?'

Another time Anna might have laughed at the wisdom of Jenny's fifteen years. Right now, she could only agree. Life without Colin Davies blowing through it like a typhoon would be a considerably smoother proposition. 'You may be right,' she smiled. 'You may be right.'

'Hey,' Jenny said, struck by a sudden thought. 'Why aren't you cooking? It is your night, isn't it?'

Anna felt an unwelcome flush creeping across her cheeks. 'Colin's making tacos,' she said, feeling guilty for, as far as she could see, no reason whatsoever.

'Aha!' Jenny shouted, triumphant. 'He is in love with you!'

'No, he just wanted tacos,' Anna denied. But she couldn't help but wonder. He had never shown any particular desire for tacos before. And fixing dinner when he knew she had been struggling with Will's research in a hot, stuffy study all day was a considerate thing to do. Damn him! Why did he have to confuse her so? Why, when she was ready to hate him, did he turn around and act considerate and thoughtful? It made it very difficult to put him in the same category as the perfidious Toby.

The kind, smiling Colin was still there at dinner. He pulled her chair out for her when she sat down at the table, and Jenny couldn't manage to smother her giggles. Between wondering what Colin was up to and trying to stifle Jenny's knowing smiles and chuckles, Anna thought she would go distracted. It was a good meal, but she couldn't get away fast enough, and she offered to wash up only because she thought that freeing Jenny from further chores might help her to vanish that much faster.

'Oh, that's okay,' Jenny said. 'You don't have to.'

'I'll help her,' Colin volunteered, and Anna wanted to die. But he shoved his chair back from the table and grinned at her, an engaging, mischievous grin that made her knees weak and her heart flutter, and she gave a helpless little shrug and carried a pile of plates into the kitchen, managing to grind her tennis shoe on Jenny's outstretched foot as she passed. It did nothing to erase the younger girl's knowing smirk.

'I can do these myself,' she told Colin when he brought in another load of dishes.

'I don't mind,' he said easily, then teased, 'Just because you didn't take pity on me and stay to talk while I was cooking, that doesn't mean I won't take pity on you.'

Pity! Is that what it was? she wondered, tying on an apron. Torment more likely. Will came in and poured himself a cup of coffee and she said quickly, 'If you want me to do more typing later, I will.' It would be a good excuse for hurrying away from the kitchen after.

'He doesn't,' Colin said.

Will raised an eyebrow, then shrugged. 'I don't,' he said equably, and Anna thought that if Colin told him horses grew on trees he would agree. Anything to keep the peace. He was a joy to work with, she wouldn't trade him, but when it came to bucking Colin, he had the backbone of a sponge.

'Well, if you should change your mind,' she offered weakly, and Colin said,

'He won't,' with just as much assurance as he had before, and Will escaped upstairs without comment.

Anna ran the water as hard as she dared and set up a terrific clatter with the dishes, scrubbing for all she was worth in an effort to ignore him. But he wouldn't be ignored. His hand shot out and flicked off the water.

'The plates were brown to begin with,' he grinned. 'Scrubbing won't change that.' His hand went up and caressed the back of her neck and she jerked away.

'Soap,' he explained. 'I was just wiping it off.' His hand continued its gentle ministrations, and shivers coursed down Anna's spine.

'That's enough,' she hissed. How could she remain indifferent to him when he was doing this? She reached up and brushed straggling wisps of hair away from her face, getting more soapsuds on her cheeks and chin as she did so.

'You look like you've been foaming at the mouth,' Colin said, wiping her face gently with the dishtowel. His dark eyes were warm and inviting, and she wondered where the angry man of the afternoon had gone. Her pulse raced as he continued to dab at the corner of her mouth, the dishtowel replaced by the tips of his fingers.

'Colin?' her voice was shaky, bewildered.

'I'm not an ogre, Anna,' he said softly, and his gaze compelled her to believe him.

She ducked her head, confused. 'Please, Colin . . .'

'Please what?'

'I—I don't know. I don't understand.' It sounded stupid, inadequate, but her mind was spinning. Images of Colin and Toby whirled madly in her head, daring her to make sense of them. In some ways he was so different from Toby. Toby was as irresponsible about his job as he had been about his personal relationships. 'Take me or leave me,' he seemed to say. But Colin, in his job anyway, was a perfectionist. If he didn't get it done right the first time, he tried again. Harder. And with his personal relationships? Anna sighed. Well, there was Cindy Tate. And herself. And plenty of other women in the past to hear Will tell it. So who knew? Who really knew?

'What are you thinking?' Colin asked, his eyes probing.

'That I don't understand you,' Anna replied honestly.

Colin chewed on his lower lip, then smiled wryly. 'I know what you mean,' he said, scratching the back of his head.

Anna looked at him quizzically.

'I'm not sure I understand myself either.'

And which Colin Davies will it be this morning? Anna wondered as she buttered her toast. It was a brightly sunny day, even hotter and more humid than the preceding one, and Anna thought it would help if he could co-ordinate his Jekyll and Hyde transformations with the weather. But it didn't seem likely. Yesterday she had seen both and the sun had shone the whole time. The nice one had lasted the rest of the evening. He had dried the dishes in silence, apparently deciding that their tenuous truce wouldn't survive too much probing or analysis. And when he had left at eight to go to some sort of meeting, he looked rather like he would have preferred to stay home with her. But maybe, she thought as she munched on her toast, that was just wishful thinking. Thinking that she couldn't indulge much longer. She had work to do today that would, she hoped redeem her for yesterday's miserable output. But the thought of sitting in that hot, airless room sent her to the stove to put on the kettle for another cup of tea.

The screen door banged and Colin appeared, rugged and appealing in a pair of faded denim cut-offs, his tanned, hair-roughened chest glistening with perspiration.

'I need reinforcements,' he announced.

'Huh?'

'I'm putting together a pot and I need help.' He brushed a dirty hand through his hair. 'Expert help. From a potter.' His eyes implored her, and his mouth twisted in a self-deprecating grin. 'I bet you thought I'd never ask,' he teased, reminding her of his earlier unwillingness to let her into any part of his work.

She grinned. 'I thought you could manage.'

He shrugged. 'Come look,' he invited. She followed him out on to the side porch where spread on the cement were heaps of small fragments of a clay pot. She couldn't help the groan of dismay.

'See?' he said. 'Bet you've never made a pot out of that before.'

'You win. It's like a puzzle without any idea of what the picture is supposed to look like at the end.'

'Well, if you don't want to help,' he began defensively, as though she had rejected him right off.

'I didn't say that,' Anna said, sitting down crosslegged, and brushing her hair back from her eyes. 'Sit down and tell me where to start.'

He sat and began to describe the pot he imagined that this one would eventually be. Anna tried to concentrate, but she was intensely aware of the firmly muscled, nearly naked body just inches from hers, and kept having to tear her mind from thoughts of him to thoughts of Mayan pots! She watched the strong, deft fingers as they manipulated pieces of the rim and remembered the feel of them on her cheek, her mouth. Stop it, she told herself firmly. Just think about the pot.

But it wasn't as easy as that. They worked harmoniously side by side for a while, neither saying much, and Anna began to relax a bit, enjoying the challenge of reconstructing the pot. But then Colin said, 'Had enough?' as though he expected her to leap up and run off at the first opportunity.

'No,' she said. 'Why? Do you want to quit?'

He shook his head. 'But that doesn't mean you can't.'

'I'm enjoying it.'

'You are?' he sounded incredulous, rather like he had when he had taken her arrowhead hunting and she had liked that. He bent his head and concentrated on a piece he was trying to fit to the rim section. 'Cindy hates it,' he said in a low voice.

Anna didn't move. She didn't say a word. She had no idea what to say. But she couldn't help the way her heart twisted inside her. Cindy. Always Cindy. How he must have loved her. How he must *still* love her!

'Do you miss California?' he asked now, changing the subject completely. Probably, Anna guessed, because he knew how much he was revealing about his feelings for Cindy.

'No. Why?'

'Just wondered. You like living in the mid west?'

'Oh yes. I love it here.'

Colin nodded. 'Me too. But I like field work too.'

'I know. It sounds fascinating. I envy you.'

Colin looked sceptical. 'Most women wouldn't.'

Cindy again, Anna thought. God, I wish I hated him. I wish I couldn't stand the sight of him. But her hands ached to touch him, to show him the love she could give him. She clenched her fingers, denying them what they wanted most. 'Maybe you're right,' she said quickly, getting to her feet. 'Maybe I do need a break. You just carry on. I'll go start on my typing for Will.' She headed for the door. 'I'll bring you some lemonade.'

Colin's expression clouded, his eyes dark unreadable. 'Go ahead,' he said dully.

He took the proffered mug without looking up, grunting his thanks, and Anna went back inside feeling that she'd been reintroduced to the first Colin, the one who managed. 'Good luck,' she said in a lighter tone than she felt, and if she heard crockery shattering as she vanished up the stairs, she only hoped it was the mug and not the Mayan pot.

Typing was useless. She filled the waste basket with error-riddled pages and told herself irritably that it was the heat causing her errors and not Colin Davies. But she wasn't fooled that easily. A week's worth of avoiding him had done absolutely no good whatsoever. One big fight and several hours of charm and he was back in her life as big as ever. He might be unreliable, unscrupulous and untrustworthy, but he was also unforgettable. All he had to do was look at her, smile, tease her, be the tiniest bit nice, and she melted. Talk about creatures without backbone, she thought. Will and I make a pair!

She tugged fretfully at the tank top which was sticking to her perspiration-soaked body. A shower sounded heavenly. She would take a quick one and then type. Being clean and cool might even help. It certainly couldn't hurt.

She ran lightly down the hall from Will's study, grabbed clean clothes from her room and congratulated herself on showering now and avoiding the evening rush when everyone wanted the shower. Then she zipped down to the bathroom, and flung open the door.

'Grand Central Station,' Colin said. He was shaving, the razor midway down his cheek, and Anna stopped stone still, staring, for the only thing he wore was a bit of lather.

'S—S—Sorry.' Her cheeks flamed, but she didn't leave. She felt as though her feet had taken root. Only her eyes moved, roving over the planes and angles of his body, savouring the broad chest, narrow hips, long, well-muscled legs.

'I'm not,' Colin replied. 'I think it's a great idea.'

'What?'

'Showering together.' He grinned.

'Don't be absurd,' Anna retorted. 'I made a mistake. I didn't know you were in here. I'll take one later.'

'No.' He shut the door, loosing her unresisting hand from the handle, pulling her towards him, his desire very evident now.

'No?' You're an idiot, Anna, she told herself, staring up into the dark, emotion-filled eyes, her breathing hard and shaky.

'No.' He clasped both of her hands, laying them

against his chest so that she could feel the rough hair, the smooth skin, the thundering of his heart. Her fingers moved gently with a will of their own, touching, stroking, tormenting, and she saw him bite his lip and felt a shudder run through him.

'God,' he muttered, dragging her against him. 'You're driving me insane.'

'Yes,' she breathed. 'Yes.' And the feeling was mutual.

He lifted his head from her hair, his eyes glazed with desire. 'Are you *trying* to?' he demanded hoarsely.

'No, of course not. It's just that I don't understand what you do to me either.' Or *why*, to be more precise.

'What do I do to you?'

Set me on fire, she wanted to say. Make me want to sing and dance, laugh and scream and cry. 'Bother me,' she said. 'Annoy me. Irritate me.'

'I make you feel alive,' he whispered. His hands slid up under her top and unfastened the clasp to her bra, moving around to cup her breasts.

'Don't,' she mumbled, but his hands moved on relentlessly, tracing patterns just as teasing as the ones she had plagued him with moments before. She dug her fingernails into his back, and he shook his head and asked thickly,

'Why not?'

'I don't want you to.' It was a lie. She wanted him to go on forever. But not after what he had said earlier. Not when he was still pining after Cindy Tate. Not when she could be just any girl—available to satisfy his momentary desire.

He nibbled on her earlobe, his warm breath causing delicious shivers to course through her body, and she trembled, thinking, I can't hold out against this much longer. 'You want it,' Colin murmured. 'We both do.'

'I—no . . .' she tried once more, however weakly, to push away from him, but her own arms were traitorous, going up to lock around his neck, pulling his head down, pressing his teasing lips against her own. She felt as though her body was about to be consumed by flames far greater than the simple bonfire emotions she had experienced with Toby, and completely beyond what she felt when kissing Rich.

Oh my God, Rich! She curled her fingers in Colin's hair, tugging his head back from hers, stepping back to put the necessary inches between them.

'Wha . . .'

'I can't,' she gasped, 'No, I forgot Rich!' She owed him some allegiance at least. Behaving like this she was no better than Colin with Cindy!

'Forget Rich,' Colin snapped. 'It's the first sensible thing you've done since you got here!' He was glaring at her, the glaze of desire in his eyes replaced by a barely disguised fury.

'Hardly,' she muttered, looking everywhere but at him, trying not to notice his very obvious arousal.

'Damn you,' Colin swore. 'When are you going to grow up?' He caught hold of her chin and forced her to look at him. 'When are you going to face what you really feel?' He snorted in disgust. 'Or maybe you never will. Maybe you're just too scared.' His hand dropped and he yanked a towel off the rack, knotting it round his hips. 'Is that it, Anna?' he goaded her, reaching for the handle and flinging open the door. 'Are you scared?' His voice was cold and implacable, full of contempt, and he didn't bother to wait for an answer, stalking down the hall to his room and slamming the door.

Scared? Anna thought, staring after him, mute in the face of his fury. You bet, I'm scared. To death. Colin had nailed it, all right. She was petrified of what would happen to her if she let down her defences, let him into her life. How could she do that knowing how he felt about Cindy Tate? Her hands shook as she undressed and turned on the cold water full blast. The icy needles took her breath away, but failed to touch the furore in her mind. Grow up, he had said. She sighed, recognising the truth in that. By growing up she had to face what she felt. And that meant stopping hiding behind her engagement to Rich. It meant, she realised, that her engagement was over. Simple as that. No, she thought, shaking her head in wry amusement. Nothing was a simple as that. The engagement might be over; her problems were just beginning.

She dried off briskly and finished dressing. There was still the little matter of Cindy Tate. Even if she was no longer engaged to Rich, that didn't mean that Colin loved her. It just meant he could say 'I told you so' when he found out, and that she couldn't use Rich as an excuse anymore when she tried to evade him. Why evade him? she asked herself. He wants you.

Yes, but can I trust him?

Only as far as I can throw him, she thought grimly. That was the problem. She walked back to her room, noting that his door was open and he was gone. Tossing her dirty clothes on the bed, she heard a car door slam and walked to the window to see who it was. Colin had just got into a Volvo—a red one. The Tates' Volvo, Anna thought, spotting a flash of blonde hair on the driver's side. Her stomach knotted. Fast work, fella, she thought, letting the curtain drop.

'Only as far as I can throw him,' she murmured, an ache in her heart. 'And maybe not even that.'

CHAPTER SEVEN

SHE spent the rest of the afternoon typing Will's notes, forcing herself to be meticulous and thorough, less because of her dedication to her job than because if she concentrated solely on the notes she avoided all thoughts of Colin. But she could push such distraction just so far, and faced with his empty chair at the dinner table, she couldn't pretend he didn't matter any longer.

'Where's Colin?' William asked, shovelling up Jenny's instant mashed potatoes.

Letting Cindy have her 'share' of him, Anna thought bitterly, and was not at all surprised to hear Jenny say,

'He called about half an hour ago. Some meeting came up and he said he would just grab a bite to eat later.'

Meeting, ha! Anna's stomach rebelled at the thought of food, but she continued chewing mechanically, hoping she'd be able to swallow when the time came.

'You've been very quiet,' Will said to her. 'Feel all right?'

'I've got a bit of a headache,' Anna replied, which was nothing but the truth. 'I'll lie down after dinner.'

'Do that. I'll wash up.'

'Gee,' Jenny said brightly, 'Maybe Will's in love with you, too. Nobody offers to do the dishes for me.'

'Too?' Will's eyebrows arched in interest.

Anna shoved back her chair and stood up, setting her water glass on her plate with a decided clank. 'Jenny has an overactive imagination,' she said, giving the younger girl a dark look. 'I hope it's just her age.' She carried her dishes to the sink and gave Will a faint smile. 'Thanks, Will. I do appreciate your offer.'

She didn't go to bed immediately, but sat down at her desk and tried to write a letter to Rich. Somehow she couldn't call him and tell him this over the 'phone. What would she say? 'Hello, I'm sorry but I've discovered that we're just not suited. I'll be returning your ring. Goodbye.' Hardly. She needed to write it all out, explain it. It would have been best to tell him face to face, but she couldn't wait until she saw him at Christmas to do it. It wouldn't, as Colin had pointed out a couple of months ago, 'be fair'. She chewed on her pen for a moment, then tore up the paper and flung it on top of the half dozen other false starts already in the wastebasket.

'Damn,' she muttered. 'Damn it all anyway.' She groaned, tossing the pen down and stretched out on her bed contemplating the cracked plaster ceiling. She'd heard of 'writer's block' but somehow she'd never imagined that it extended to situations like this! Perhaps if she slept on it, took a nap for an hour or so, she would make a better job of it later. A nice excuse anyway, she congratulated herself, and feeling only somewhat guilty, she rolled over and hugged her pillow for comfort, refusing to move until sleep overtook her.

She didn't know how much later it was when Jenny opened the door a crack. 'If you're awake, there's a call for you,' she said.

'Who?' Anna dragged herself to a sitting position, her body as responsive as lead.

'Rich.'

It wasn't even Tuesday night, Anna thought groggily. Something must be wrong. 'Tell him I'll be right there.'

The door to Colin's room opened and he came out, looking after her curiously, but she brushed past him, murmuring, 'Excuse me, please,' and grabbed the telephone.

'Hello,' she said breathlessly. 'What's wrong?'

'Nothing.' Rich's voice was calm and reassuring. 'Good news.'

'What?'

'I'm flying to Chicago on Thursday. Can you meet me there?'

'Thursday?' she echoed stupidly, a stone where her stomach used to be. 'Oh, uh, well, uh, yes. Sure. I suppose. I'll take a bus in.'

'Can't you fly?'

'Too expensive.'

'I'll pay for it.'

'No, really. I'd prefer the bus.' She knew her insistence irritated him, but he didn't argue.

'I'll meet you at the bus station then.'

Anna thought how out of place Rich would look—and feel—at the bus station. 'No, stay at your hotel. I'll come there. Where are you staying?'

'The Palmer House.'

It figured. 'I'll be there,' she promised.

'Terrific.' Just the sound of his voice comforted her. She didn't want to let him go, especially not when she could see Colin, poised to spring, hovering on the stairs. But finally she had to say, 'See you on Thursday,' and hang up. At least it solved one problem. Now she could tell him in person.

'Where are you going with him?' Colin demanded as she went back to open the door of her room.

'What business is it of yours?'

'Everybody here thinks you're engaged to me.'

'So what? Rich is my real fiancé. And I'm going to meet him in Chicago on Thursday.' She knew she sounded like a defiant child, but she couldn't help it. He always brought out the worst in her.

'I'll drive you.'

'You will not!'

'We can tell everyone we're going to Chicago for the day.'

'No. I'm going alone.'

Colin just shook his head, not saying anything, managing by just his manner to look smug and superior and as though she didn't know her own mind.

'Leave me alone, Colin Davies,' she said, whirling away from him. 'I don't even like you.'

'Hang on a minute, lady,' he grated, catching her before she could enter her room, spinning her around to face him. 'That isn't the impression I got. Not long ago you couldn't keep your hands off me.'

'Let me go,' she said, struggling against the arms

which imprisoned her against him, but he was too strong to be moved. Then, without warning, his hands dropped.

'All right, go. But don't think you're going to Chicago without me because you're not!' He spun away and went into his own room, slamming the door so hard that Anna felt her teeth rattle. Was that a threat, she wondered, staring after him, or a promise? He was certainly confusing lately. One minute he acted like he wanted to ravish her, and the next he was storming out of the house. And then there was Cindy Tate.

'Are you quite sure he isn't in love with you?' Jenny asked, peering out of her own room, obviously ready to duck at any moment.

'There's a laugh,' Anna said huskily, feeling a bit dizzy with the turn of events. She thought vaguely that she could do with Rich right now. Someone calm and rational sounded like the perfect tonic. And she clearly needed one.

Thursday morning Anna awoke eager and apprehensive at the same time, whether because of what she had to tell Rich or because of a possible confrontation with Colin she didn't care to analyse. She took special care dressing, pulling her hair back into a loose chignon, and putting on a pastel rainbow shirtwaist dress that she thought made her look woman-about-town-ish without being too dressy for a long bus trip. She had asked Will to take her to the bus depot at supper last night, and she went downstairs shortly before six, expecting to see him because the light in the kitchen was already on. But it was Colin who was sitting at the table eating toast and drinking coffee.

'Where's Will?'

'Sleeping. Marta Fernandez called me last night. She was on my expedition until last Easter. I'm going in to meet her at the Field Museum today. I'll just run you in too since I've got to go anyway.' He looked very assured and matter-of-fact, saying this all offhandedly, though she was certain he had contrived the whole meeting.

'To Chicago, you mean?' she asked, wanting to get it straight.

'Yeah.'

'That won't be necessary. The bus station is quite as far as I want to go with you.'

'God. You are the most infuriating woman. I am not driving to Chicago by myself while you ride the bus behind me.'

'I don't want to go with you.'

'What are you afraid of?' he asked mockingly. 'Me? Or yourself?'

'Neither. I just don't want to.' She knew how weak it sounded.

'Prove you're not afraid,' Colin said evenly. 'Ride with me.' He shoved back his chair and stood, looming over her, looking disturbingly attractive in the light blue slacks, oxford cloth shirt, and the blue and burgundy striped tie that he had worn the night he took her out to dinner. The recollection didn't do anything to dampen her ardour, she thought wryly. He would make her pulses jump no matter what he was wearing—or wasn't. She turned pink at the thought and looked down at the coffee cup she was holding, too embarrassed at the direction of her thoughts to meet his eyes.

'Be out in ten minutes,' Colin said abruptly and went back upstairs.

Bossy cad, Anna thought. I ought to get a bus just to spite him. But she wouldn't, she knew, because there was no one else to take her with Will sleeping, and he would think she was crazy if she wanted to ride the bus when Colin was going anyway. Will didn't know yet that his early warning about Colin's tendency towards no commitments had done no good at all, that in spite of knowing that he only wanted a brief fling, Anna had fallen in love with him anyway.

She had thought that the drive was going to be difficult, and she wasn't wrong. Not because they sniped at each other or because Colin mocked her and she squirmed. In fact they were both on their best behaviour, and that was perhaps the most difficult thing of all. They very carefully skirted every controversial issue, never mentioning Cindy Tate or their own mock engagement or even Anna's purpose in going to Chicago. They tiptoed carefully through conversations about the weather, baseball, teaching school, tourist sights in Chicago and, when anything remotely personal came up, they gave it wide berth. Consequently they reached the outskirts of the city without tearing each other to shreds, but Anna felt as though she had been wrung out just the same. She could hardly wait until the ordeal was over.

'Where can I take you?' Colin asked.

'I'm meeting him at the Palmer House,' Anna said, and Colin's jaw tightened but he didn't comment, just nodded, and she thought that the truce just might hold until they got there. She hoped he would just drop her on a street corner and give her directions, but there was little chance of that.

'I want to meet him,' Colin said flatly when she suggested it. 'I want to see what the competition is.'

'There is no competition. I'm engaged to Rich.' He didn't need to know that she was breaking it off. But Colin parked the car in a crowded and very expensive parking garage and grabbed her arm, tugging her along the sidewalks and up the steps to the lobby of the Palmer House. 'Come on,' he said tersely.

'I am not a piece of baggage,' Anna said, jerking her arm away from him. But he grasped her hand just as firmly, twining her fingers in his strong ones, and led her on.

The Palmer House reminded her of Rich's apartment décor—all green and gold and lots of marble. Elegant and expensive, but impersonal, though Rich also managed to look more contemporary. In any case, both were a far cry from the homey comfort she was used to at Fieldings'. She felt distinctly out of place here, but a quick glance in a full length mirror as Colin dragged her past showed her that she looked all right and that

Colin fitted in perfectly. He could look just as wealthy and executive as anyone when he wanted to, she realised, glancing up at the man by her side. The stiff breeze had tossed his hair into disarray, but it only added a certain casual boyishness to his otherwise hard, businesslike demeanour. They were approaching the desk to get Rich's room number when she heard a voice say,

'Anna?' and she turned to see Rich rising up out of one of the forest green overstuffed chairs. He came towards her smiling, and she said,

'How very good to see you,' and they kissed and she never felt a thing.

Rich drew back and looked at her appraisingly, then seemed to notice Colin for the first time. 'Who is——' he waved his hand in Colin's direction. Anna blushed furiously, realising that not only had she been noticeably indifferent to his kiss but that Colin still had a hold of her hand.

'This,' she said, tugging to get free, but Colin was having none of it, 'is Dr Colin Davies, Dr Fielding's cousin.' She wished he looked old and ill, the way Rich must have been picturing him, instead of so disgustingly attractive, virile and healthy.

'Oh.' Rich was nonplussed, but only for a moment. 'Pleased to meet you,' he said, recovering quickly and giving Colin a genuine smile and hand shake.

'You, too,' Colin replied, shaking the hand offered while scrutinising Rich with as much careful interest as Rich was showing him. They reminded Anna of two dogs warily circling each other, looking out for signs of weakness.

'Colin came in to meet with a colleague of his at the Field Museum,' Anna found herself explaining rapidly to paper over the awkwardness she felt. 'And I thought it was ridiculous to ride the bus if he was coming anyway.'

'Of course,' Rich said smoothly. 'Thank you very much for seeing her here, Dr Davies. Now, if you'll excuse us——'

'Where can I pick you up?' Colin said to Anna abruptly, ignoring Rich's dismissal.

'Oh, I——'

'I'll see her back to Belle River,' Rich said.

'Rich that's a four-hour drive,' Anna began, then thought, What am I complaining about?

'I can rent a car.'

'No need. I'll bring her back with me,' Colin cut in smoothly. 'No problem.'

Like a parcel, Anna thought. Rich hesitated. 'Is it really four hours?'

'More or less,' Anna said.

'More,' Colin told him blithely. Anna glared at him.

'Still, I can spare the time,' Rich decided.

'Why don't we meet for a beer about four o'clock at Berghoff's and you can decide then,' Colin suggested. 'You'll have a better idea by that time.'

A better idea of what? Anna wondered. Of how much they could stand of one another by then?

'All right,' Rich agreed and, nodding to Colin, he took Anna's arm and led her to the elevator. She glanced over her shoulder, but Colin had disappeared. She saw only the ends of his coat-tails as he went around the corner. As if he couldn't wait to get away and spend the day with Marta Fernandez, whoever she was. Another of his flings perhaps?

'I have a meeting at eleven-thirty in the John Hancock building,' Rich was saying. 'How would you like to shop at Water Tower Place while I'm at the meeting and then we'll have lunch after at the Ritz?'

Lunch at the Ritz, Anna mused. How she had missed Rich saying things like that! They were so normal in his world and had become so foreign to hers. 'If you want to,' she said offhandedly as he helped her into the taxi, and then regretted not showing more enthusiasm. After all, Rich was trying to make her happy and he was the man she had been planning to marry.

'Your Dr Davies was quite a surprise,' he said when they were underway.

Anna pulled back instinctively. I wondered when we'd get to that, she thought and wished it had not been so soon. 'He not *my* Dr Davies,' she protested. 'He's just staying at the Fieldings' until he's well enough to go back to Guatemala.'

'I would have said he looked damned healthy.'

'Now, yes. You should have seen him two months ago,' Anna said and immediately wished she'd kept her mouth shut.

'He's been around *that* long?'

'Yes. He was in the hospital quite a long while.'

'Well, he's made a remarkable recovery.'

'Do we have to talk about him?' Anna asked. 'I haven't seen you since June. Surely we have other things to say.'

'Of course,' Rich agreed, and proceeded to tell her all about Teri Gibbs. 'She says I need looking after,' Rich told her, a twist of amusement in his smile. 'She thinks you were crazy to go off and leave me "unattended". Her word.'

'I'm sure she's taking remarkably good care of you,' Anna said, surprised at how little she cared that Teri had taken over this way.

'She is. She makes marvellous veal scallopini.' He closed his eyes as if the thought of it gave him many happy moments. Anna thought, there is more to this than veal scallopini. 'She got the tar stain out of my white jeans,' he went on.

A veritable paragon, Anna thought. Teri had facets Anna had never dreamed of. 'Did she? How clever.'

Rich smiled. 'Here we are,' he announced as the cab drew up in front of Marshall Field's on Michigan Avenue. 'I'll see you in and we can decide where to meet.'

After they had entered the seven storey shopping centre with its glass elevators and elegantly appointed shops, Anna pointed to a cosy French bakery and said, 'How about there? Then whichever of us arrives first won't starve.'

'Perfect. One o'clock?' He bent his head and kissed her on the lips. For an instant a lean, dark face intruded on her thoughts. But then she blinked her eyes fiercely and saw instead Rich's wide blue eyes smiling down at her from beneath neatly combed blond hair. 'See you at one,' he repeated softly, turned on his heel and disappeared.

It was nearly that when Anna, carrying several small parcels, got to the bakery. Rich was nowhere to be seen. She waited until a booth was available and ordered a cup of coffee and an almond croissant, nibbling at it as she wondered how she was going to break the news to Rich. It was a nice place to wait—an opportunity to watch a crossways slice of life, seeing a sliver of so many peoples' daily activities, the things they bought and used. Very archaeological, Colin would have said, this business of trying to find out about peoples' lives from observing their artefacts. And what better place to do that than a shopping mall? She wondered what it would be like to dig one up in several thousand years and try to determine what the twentieth century valued. She would have liked to have asked Colin what he thought.

'Been waiting long?' Rich slid into the chair across from her, and a waiter appeared as if by magic to take his order. 'Just coffee,' he said and a cup appeared instantly. That was how it was with Rich, Anna thought. Waiters, taxis and doormen popped out as soon as they saw him coming. He had a sort of presence that scared her at times, as if he expected everything to happen just when he wanted it to—and it did. With Rich life would be all clockwork, no guesswork, and Anna found it intimidating. She had forgotten just how much.

'How was your meeting?' she asked him.

'Good, but I'm afraid I'll have to let Dr Davies take you home. They want me to attend a party tonight. Do you mind?'

'No.' She could cope with Colin, she would have to.

'He won't bother you, will he?'

'What do you mean?' She knew exactly what he meant.

'He seemd to think he owned you.'

'He doesn't.'

'Keep reminding him. You're my fiancée.'

'Mmmmm.' It was an opening, but she couldn't take it. Drama on an empty stomach was not her style.

'Shall we go over to the Ritz now?'

'I found a lovely little Mexican restaurant here,' Anna told him. 'I haven't had any good Mexican food since I left LA. How about going there?'

'How do you know it'll be any good? You can trust the Ritz.'

'I know. But let's be a little adventurous.' She looked at him pleadingly, not something she usually did. She had always been in the habit of doing whatever Rich wanted.

Rich looked rather like he did mind, but he wasn't going to refuse her, not after two months' separation. 'All right,' he acquiesced. 'Lead on. But if I get indigestion, you're to blame.'

It was a cheerful restaurant, and Rich perked up immediately when he saw it. The waitress there was equally prompt about finding them a table, and Rich ordered them both sangria while they waited for their lunches. The drink was heady, and Anna wasn't sure she needed it in the middle of the day. Just sitting there with Rich across the table was enough to confuse her. It was is if the two intervening months had given them nothing to talk about. She watched him over a basket of warm tortilla chips as he talked about the meeting he had just left and she thought, Richard Howell, you are handsome and well-informed, conscientious and undeniably attractive. Also, you make me feel warm, secure and comfortable. So why doesn't *your* gaze set me on fire? Why do I feel sleepy rather than strung up in your presence? Why on earth wasn't it *you* who made me realise how dead all my feelings have been since Toby instead of Colin Davies?

'. . . get the recipe,' Rich finished.

'What?' Anna blushed. 'I'm sorry, I must have been dreaming.'

'I said Teri makes great goulash too. You must get the recipe.'

'Yes, I will.' She munched on a tortilla chip and mused about that. She would probably never cook as well as Teri did if she tried for fifty years. She probably wouldn't get stains out of the knees of his jeans either, or charm the boss's wife. 'Teri is a great girl,' she said firmly, seeing an opening she liked. 'She'd make a wonderful wife.' She wanted to say, she's miles more suitable for you than I am.

'Yes,' Rich agreed thoughtfully as if he were considering this for the first time. 'She would. Did you want me to fix her up with someone?'

'Well,' Anna looked over his shoulder at the *papier maché* sculpture of a bull's head on the opposite wall. 'Someone like you, perhaps.'

'Like me?'

'She'd make a good wife for someone like you,' Anna insisted. 'She knows what to say at parties, she makes great veal scallopini, she could keep your clothes clean.' She looked at him hopefully. 'You know what I mean.'

'I'm beginning to.' Rich studied the bottom of his glass as though he were fascinated by it. Then he looked at her squarely. 'Are you trying to tell me you're returning my ring?' he asked gently.

'I—If—If you want, yes.' Anna looked down at her napkin twisted in her fingers.

'Is it because of Colin Davies?'

'No!' Was it *that* obvious?

'He wishes it were,' Rich said drily, setting his glass down with a thump.

'What?'

'He wouldn't act like a guard dog otherwise.'

'That's just the way he is—arrogant, touchy. He's used to bossing me.' Before she realised it she found herself telling Rich what had been happening over the past two months. Without knowing exactly how it happened she fell into the old pattern of sharing things with him as a friend shares with another friend. Their relationship suddenly felt right again, the way it had before they had got engaged. Just friends, no pressure.

'You do understand, don't you?' she pleaded when

she had finished and was searching his face for a sign that he felt the same way she did.

Rich smiled a little wryly. 'Yes, I suppose I do. To be honest, you are quite right. Teri would make a good wife for someone like me.'

'Will you ask her?' Anna demanded, wanting to know that he would be happy.

'Oh, Anna,' he laughed. 'I don't hop from one engagement to the next! You know me better than that.'

'But you do see that *I'm* not right?' she persisted. How could he miss it, she wondered. He wouldn't hop from one engagement to another while she managed to get 'engaged' to two men at once!

'If you say so.'

'I do. I'd embarrass you every other minute.'

'What about Davies? Won't you embarrass him?'

'I don't think it's possible. But if I did it would serve him right for the way he's been using me. Anyway,' she sighed, 'he's a love 'em and leave 'em type. No commitments, according to Will.'

'Not like me.'

Anna shook her head and gave him a small wistful smile. 'No. More's the pity. Not at all like you.'

'We'll have to shape him up then,' Rich said, cutting off a piece of enchilada and taking a bite.

'What? How?' She could scarcely believe what she was hearing.

Rich shrugged, a definite twinkle in his eyes. 'Simple. Don't tell him you've broken the engagement yet.'

Anna's eyes widened. 'You mean . . .'

'It's the lawyer in me.' Rich grinned as wicked a grin as she could ever remember seeing on him. 'He obviously expects you to end it all with me today. Then he'll be around to pick up the pieces and have this Cindy girl too. He doesn't strike me as a fool. He can see we don't suit, especially if he's been hanging around you for the last two months.'

'What do you mean " he can see we don't suit"? We were engaged, for heaven's sake, up until ten minutes ago! We didn't see that we didn't suit!'

'Didn't we? So why did you run off to Belle River then?'

'Well, I——' She couldn't meet his eyes.

'Exactly. You felt awkward, uncomfortable, and at times, I admit, so did I. It was a nice idea, Anna. Don't get me wrong. I loved you. I still do in my way. But you were right to leave because it made me see that while I was in love with bits of you, other bits drove me right round the bend.' He grinned apologetically. 'You tried and so did I. We tried too damned hard. And I think we're both smart enough to realise when trying isn't enough. Aren't we?'

Anna laughed, delighted, wanting to throw her arms around him and kiss him. Only Rich could be so instantly reasonable and rational about something she had agonised over for months! He was saying everything she had wanted to say since she had left LA, everything she knew in her heart but had been afraid to articulate. God love him, with his lawyer's gift for elocution he could get it all out for her and, miracle of miracles, not resent her for it.

'Yes, Rich, we are smart enough,' she agreed solemnly, slipping the ring off her finger and handing it to him. 'I do love you, you know.'

He laughed aloud. 'First time I've ever had my ring returned by a woman saying she loved me.' He shook his head, sliding the ring back on her finger. 'You keep it. I gave it to you. I want you to have it to remember me by. Use it for now to keep Davies in line.'

'Are you serious?'

'Absolutely. I suppose I'll always regret that I didn't make it to being your husband. But I would like to think that I helped you control the one you get.'

'Colin Davies isn't likely to be my husband either.' Not to mention the fact that no one controlled Colin.

'Maybe not. But he's not uninterested. And neither are you.'

'He wants a fling.'

'So give him one.' Rich winked. 'Drink up and we'll go back to Berghoff's and meet him.'

They window shopped and wandered in and out of exclusive stores as they walked back down Michigan Avenue, thoroughly enjoying each other's company, laughing and relaxed. Anna marvelled that the day turned out so well.

'I can't believe it,' she said to Rich, and when he cocked his head quizzically, she added, 'That we're still friends, I mean.'

'Of course.' He took her hand and squeezed it, holding it in his as they continued to walk, and Anna thought how lucky she was to have learned that he was her friend just in time. She'd have never felt like this if she had married him.

Colin was already drinking a beer at the bar when they entered. The dimly lit, oak panelled walls created an instant warmth that mirrored the surge that Anna felt when she saw him. Infuriating, prickly, arrogant man that he was, she couldn't help herself. She loved him. Even Rich didn't doubt it. But always there was Cindy, and Colin's own reluctance to make another commitment. She felt Rich slip his arm around her shoulders, tugging her closer to him. His mouth brushed her ear. 'Give me a kiss,' he commanded.

She turned her head and saw the light of laughter in his eyes. 'I didn't know you were so wicked,' she said. He was more daring than she could have supposed. She reached up and brushed her lips lightly across his, then turned back to see Colin glaring at them.

'Been waiting long?' She gave him a sweet smile that he didn't return.

'No.' He swallowed the rest of his beer in one gulp and motioned for another plus one for each of them. 'What'd you decide?' he asked Rich.

'I'm afraid I'll have to ask you to take Anna back tonight after all,' Rich said with obvious reluctance. 'I have to go to a party I can't miss.'

Colin shrugged. 'Whatever you want.' He didn't look overjoyed. Maybe Rich had read too much into his 'guard dog' attitude earlier.

'Did you see your colleague?' Anna asked him.

'Yeah.'

'Was it important?'

'It could be.'

She wanted to kick him. How could he stand there like a stone and ignore her? Especially after he had made such a big deal about coming along and about taking her home after. Rich, however, who was proving that he had more subtlety in his little finger than she had in her whole body, gave Colin a broad conspiratorial grin and said, 'We had a fantastic day! Didn't we, darling?' His eyes moved possessively over Anna.

Colin looked up then, his features set in grim lines as he stared at Anna, his eyes narrowing as if she were the villain of the piece. 'Did you now?' he asked, sarcasm dripping.

'Yes, lovely,' she said blithely, stifling a giggle. The beer shouldn't be having such an effect on her, she thought. But she desperately wanted to discomfit him somehow. He had done it to her often enough, and he was always so bossy and self-assured.

'If you're ready we'd better go then,' he said flatly. 'I want to get out of here before dark.'

'So soon?' Anna looked soulfully at Rich and his mouth quirked in amusement. She thought, I could do this professionally. Why didn't I ever consider acting as a career?

'We could have supper first,' Rich suggested.

'No, I want to get going.' Colin finished his glass of beer and straightened up, brushing a hand through windswept, dark hair. His eyes were on Anna, following her every movement until she felt she was a bug under glass, a highly disapproved of bug under glass.

'All right,' she sighed. 'If you say so.' She picked up her handbag and her parcels and put her hand on Rich's arm. Then she turned to Colin. 'Could you give us a minute alone for our goodbyes?' she asked.

Colin clamped his teeth together as though he might explode, but then he nodded curtly and moved towards the door, shooting her a withering glance over his shoulder which she pretended to ignore.

'I wouldn't want to be in his shoes,' Rich said softly, putting his hands on her shoulders and drawing her against him.

'Why?'

'I always figured you were fierce when aroused. Now I know.'

'You're a dear, Rich. Not everyone would put up with me.'

He grinned. 'True enough. Invite me to the wedding.'

'I doubt there'll be one.'

'I wouldn't bet on it.'

'It's all a game to him. You know, a dalliance, an affair. I told you about Cindy. He just wants a good time.'

'He isn't having one now,' Rich said because he had a clear view of Colin as he stood impatiently by the door, his face averted as he studiously examined blown-up photos of turn-of-the-century Chicago.

'Thanks for everything,' Anna whispered and kissed Rich lightly. She was astonished when he wrapped his arms around her and his lips bruised hers. When at last he let her go she stared up at him, amazed, and he winked.

'That'll give him something to think about,' he said.

'Oh, you!' she burst out laughing, and he said,

'Shhhh! How romantic is that?' So she shushed, and he gave her another quick hug before they walked over to Colin. He was staring at her, his face totally expressionless, as though it had been wiped clean of whatever emotions he was feeling.

'Nice meeting you, Colin,' Rich said, shaking his hand. 'You take good care of my girl now.'

Anna's eyes widened at his audacity, and Colin gripped her arm none too gently, promising, 'Oh, I will,' in a terse voice as he jerked her away down the street.

The moment they were out of Rich's view he pressed her up against the display window of a shoe store and ground out, 'How on earth can you be such a damned fool?' His chest was heaving against her package-laden arms.

'What?'

'How can you still be engaged to him? How can you marry him? For God's sake, how?' His voice rose to a near shout, and Anna saw several passers-by glance their way before scurrying on. 'Look, he's a charmer, I'll agree,' Colin went on, not moderating his tones a bit. 'But you're a spitfire—impulsive, volatile, fierce. Definitely not a smoothie. God, you'll die trying to be his idea of the perfect corporate wife!' He ended on a shout and Anna thought it was lucky they were in Chicago not Belle River where such a display would have drawn far more than a backward glance.

'What do you know about it?' she defended herself, glaring up at him. 'When did you become such an authority on marriage?'

'I don't need to be an authority. I've got eyes!'

'And a mouth! The biggest one I've ever seen!' Anna retorted. 'What gives you the right to tell me whom I ought to marry? Who the hell do you think you are?' It would be different if he wanted her for himself, but marriage wasn't his long suit either.

'At least I appreciate you the way you are,' he snapped, his grip on her arms hurting so that she struggled against him which only seemed to incense him more. 'I never wanted you cut out of a mould—the perfect corporate wife.'

'All you ever wanted was to use me!'

'No!'

'Yes! Leave me alone!' She jerked away from him and began to run down the street, dodging through the hordes of rush-hour pedestrians as best she could until she reached their car in the parking garage. Slumping against it she gasped for breath, wishing there was any other way to get back to Belle River than sharing a car with Colin.

He came up the stairs and took the key out of his pocket, taking her packages and stowing them in the boot before going to open the door for her. He looked dour and withdrawn, but his eyes still sparked with an undefinable rage. 'You're making a mistake,' he told her coldly. 'Can't you see that?'

She had. So had Rich. But what right had Colin to boss her around? He might be jealous as Rich had suggested, but he didn't really care about her either. He only wanted her to satisfy his own desires. He didn't want a commitment any more than Toby had.

'Do you care?' she asked him, trying to keep all emotion out of her voice.

The silence that hung between them was tangible. The noise of car horns, grinding gears and elevated trains might as well not have existed as she stared up into his usually dark but now oddly ashen face, seeing the furrows in his forehead, the dark, pulled-together brows, the confused emotions that flickered across his face.

'Yes,' he said finally, quietly, as though the fight had suddenly gone out of him. 'Yes, I think I do.' Then his hands slipped around her to lock behind her, pressing her between the car door and his hard body so that she felt all his tension and his desire. Mindlessly she felt her arms go around him, caressing the taut muscles of his back while he sought her lips. This kiss differed completely from their previous ones. Those had been warm and tender or fiery and probing. This one was simply desperate. He was like a man who had reached the end of his tether—she felt everything, the frustration, anger, aching, need in his firm lips and tense body, and she was shaken to the very core.

'Damn,' he muttered, anguished. 'Damn you.' And he thrust her away from him, jerking open the car door. He practically shoved her inside before going around and getting in behind the wheel. Grinding the gears into reverse, he backed the car out and paid the attendant. His face was harsh, stony, unyielding. Anna watched him, wondering at the turmoil in him, waiting for him to say something else, wanting him to explain.

But she waited in vain. He was silent as a Trappist and drove like a maniac all the way home.

CHAPTER EIGHT

'You heard me,' Colin said with barely disguised impatience. 'I'm going back to Guatemala.'

That was what she thought he had said, but she couldn't believe it. She had come downstairs hoping that things would be better this morning, that his anger of the day before would have subsided sufficiently so that they could have a fresh start, a start during which she could begin to convince him that what he felt for her was more than just a passing fancy so that then she could feel brave enough to confess she was no longer engaged to Rich. But the first thing he said to her as he hung up the 'phone was, 'I'm leaving. Going back to Guatemala,' and now he was repeating it.

'Why?' she demanded, stunned, sinking into a chair and staring at his grim face. It reminded her very much of the first time she had seen him, ill and angry and looking for all the world like Goldilocks' father bear.

'I'm wasting time here,' he snapped. 'Besides, there's been some looting on the site we've been excavating. If I wait much longer there may not be a site to go back to.'

'Says who?'

'Marta Fernandez. She heard from one of the Guatemalans we were working with. I talked to him yesterday on the 'phone and he confirmed it.'

'You didn't say anything yesterday.'

Colin turned his back and opened the refrigerator, rummaging inside it. 'Yesterday you had other things on your mind,' he said roughly, taking out the orange juice and banging it down on the table.

Like getting unengaged, Anna agreed silently. Like throwing over the most decent man I've ever known because, damn it, I'm in love with you! She gritted her teeth, her hands clenching around the coffee mug so tightly she thought it might shatter. A fat lot of good it did her, too. He was obviously everything she had feared he would be—ready to have a jolly old affair one minute, and quite willing to drop it if something else came along that suited him better. Shades of Toby. So much for Rich and his ideas of keeping Colin in line!

'Anyway, I'm telling you now,' he went on coldly. 'Not that you give a damn. I'm sure you'll only be too glad to see the back of me.'

Not always, Anna thought, but right now it can't happen a moment too soon. She was tempted to say so, but the 'phone rang and she smiled tightly. Saved by the bell, she went to answer it.

'Is that you, Annie?' the voice purred when she answered, and Anna felt her stomach muscles clench. 'Is Colin there? It's urgent. You don't mind, do you?'

Anna held out the receiver as though it were contaminated. 'It's Cindy,' she spat.

Colin glowered, then yanked it out of her hand. His mouth curved into a smile and his tone completely changed. 'Hi Cindy, what's up?'

Anna muttered something under her breath that she was glad he couldn't hear and went to dump her dishes into the sink. Colin was saying, 'Sure, why not? Pick you up in half an hour. No trouble at all,' and smiling at Anna with a smugness that made her want to fling the dishcloth at him. He hung up and slanted her a mocking glance. 'I'm driving in to Dubuque for a while. Cindy is coming to do some shopping. I don't suppose, as my pseudo-fiancée, you'd like to come along?'

'And share you?' Anna snapped. 'No thanks. Cindy's welcome to every bit!'

'That's right, I forgot,' he grated. 'You have Rich.' His voice was icy and his eyes glittered with remembered anger. Anna turned and fled, aware only of her own confusion.

She refused to sit by and watch while he drove off with Cindy. It would take far more will power than she possessed. So she left before he did, hopping into her VW and, grinding the gears with a ferocity that made

Will flinch where he stood under the apple tree, she drove off in a cloud of dust and gravel.

Initially she had no idea of her direction. She just wanted to get away. But she thought afterwards that subconsciously she must have had a destination in mind. Before she realised it she was turning off the highway on to the gravel road that led past Eiler's cow pasture and through the wooded hills to Salty's gate. Passing the place where she first met Cindy Tate she smiled bitterly. Little had she known then how much her life would change after that night!

With grim determination she forced her mind on to other things—the upcoming school year, the beauty of the Wisconsin countryside at the height of summer— and wound down through the woods and across the low bridge and into Salty's front yard.

Salty himself didn't seem to be around, and she felt oddly relieved. She needed the peace his house could give, but she wasn't sure she needed anyone to share it with. Her mind wanted sorting out badly, and she hoped she could do it here. She left her purse in the car and went up on the front porch, settling herself on the oak swing that hung there. The swing creaked beneath her, the rocking rhythm comforting, and Salty's spaniels whined in the house, but she ignored them because she knew that if she let them out she might spend the day chasing them, and she had enough to worry about without that.

Guatemala? She could hardly believe it even now. Talk about tossing a spanner in the works! And just when she was ready to begin her campaign to convince him he loved her. She shook her head, disbelieving. Maybe she should have told him last night that she wasn't engaged to Rich anymore. Perhaps it had been nothing but her stupid pride that hadn't allowed her to say, You were right. She grimaced, still unable to face the mocking smile and the 'I told you so' that she knew would be forthcoming. And anyway, she certainly wouldn't tell him now—not when he was going to saunter off to Guatemala as if all his kisses were nothing more than time-fillers to take the place of something he would rather have been doing. Which was what? Digging up Mayan ruins? Or making love to Cindy Tate? A good question. But whatever the answer, one thing was obvious: his interest in Anna Douglas came in a very poor third. She groaned and dragged herself off the swing, walking towards the horse barn where she leaned against the fence and watched the horses.

'Thought it was you,' a voice said behind her, and she turned to see Salty coming out of the barn. He wore overalls and a dusty straw hat, his white hair peeking out where the hat settled over his ears, and Anna had a hard time believing that he was the same man who wore three piece suits in the library.

'You don't mind?' she asked.

'Of course not. Colin's always welcome. You are, too.'

'Thanks.'

He came over to lean on the fence beside her, standing quietly just watching the horses. 'He with you?' Salty asked after a time.

He haunts me, Anna thought. He's with me everywhere. 'No,' she said. 'He's going back to Guatemala.'

Salty chewed on his thumbnail, considering. Then he asked, 'You going with him?'

'Me?' The idea tempted as much as it shocked. If only she could. If only he'd want her to. 'I—I teach,' she said lamely. 'I couldn't. Besides,' she went on more bravely, 'I don't think he feels that way about me.'

'Mmmmm,' Salty murmured, not taking his eyes off the horses. The essence of 'no comment' without saying a word, Anna reflected wryly. But then Salty remarked conversationally, 'Some people are like horses,' and she looked at him curiously. 'That one there—Gypsy,' he indicated a handsome bay with a white blaze, 'someone mistreated him way back. More than once, I'd say. He was no bargain when I got him. Took me forever to get near him. And when I did he threw me.' Salty chuckled.

'Also more than once.' He whistled, short and sharp, and the bay whickered and trotted over to him. Salty reach out and stroked his head.

'He's lovely,' Anna breathed, but her mind was less on the horse than on what Salty was saying.

'Isn't he?' A smile lit Salty's features, and he fished in his overalls pocket and came up with a candy bar. He broke it in two and gave one half to Anna, feeding the other to Gypsy. 'Only he wasn't always so lovely. He was a colossal pain in the neck. Frankly, I didn't much want to get back on after he'd tossed me off four or five times. I didn't trust him not to throw me any more than he trusted me not to hurt him.' Gypsy was nosing around Salty's pockets, looking for more candy bars, and Salty shoved his head away, still smiling. 'G'wan! Away with you!'

'He seems to trust you now.'

'He does.'

'How'd you do it?' She smiled. 'Candy bars?' It was a nice idea, but she didn't see it working with Colin.

Salty grinned. 'Nope. I'm just more stubborn than he is. I outlasted him.' He shot her a speaking glance. 'And I loved him.'

Anna gave a rueful sigh. 'It sounds easy when you talk about it.'

Salty shook his head. 'It isn't. He was a stubborn horse. He was hurt and he didn't know I wasn't going to hurt him again. Just like your Colin.'

'He's not *my* Colin,' Anna protested.

'He could be,' Salty said, but then Salty didn't know that Colin was still involved with Cindy.

'What did you mean about him being hurt? Cindy Tate?'

'Not entirely. She was just another example of what had happened to him all his life.'

'What happened to him all his life?' Colin had never talked about his childhood or his family. She only knew that Salty had taken him arrowhead hunting, that he had spent most vacations with Will's family, and that he hadn't wanted to go to the hospital when he was twelve years old. Hardly substantial by anyone's reckoning.

'People walked out on him,' Salty said simply. 'His mother left for good when he was eight. And I gather she wasn't around much even before that. His father was in the diplomatic service and really couldn't be bothered with a little boy. He had one or two stepmothers along the way who didn't have a much longer track record than his own mother, and who never took much of an interest in him anyway. He used to spend school vacations with the Fieldings. Will's mother, Hannah, is Colin's father's sister. She never minded having an extra child, but it isn't the same for a child. At least, though, he was always welcome there. And here with me.'

Anna closed her eyes in pain, her mind seeing a much younger Colin, hurt and alone, experiencing a very different childhood from her own warm, loving family upbringing. Thank God for the rough edges, she thought. Thank God for the belligerence and the spiky nature, for without them a sensitive child might easily have been crushed by the indifference. 'I didn't know,' she whispered.

'I didn't imagine you would,' Salty said. 'He doesn't talk about his parents. Doesn't want much to do with them, which is natural, I suppose. His mother drops in and out of his life, and his father calls now and then, but they're neither one of them any more dependable than the weatherman.' He looked at her steadily. 'Other than Hannah and Mac, Colin's not seen many examples of a loving marriage. You can't blame him for being sceptical.'

'He said he wasn't interested,' Anna argued, remembering Colin's disparaging remarks about never getting engaged again.

'And Gypsy didn't take kindly to me in his life either at first,' Salty retorted, and then rubbed his backside reflectively. 'And I sure had plenty of moments when I wasn't all that fond of him. We fought every step of the way.'

Anna sighed and stuffed her hands into her pockets. 'It's a pity about candy bars,' she said. 'It'd be so much simpler.'

Salty laughed and gave her a quick hug. 'Wouldn't it?' he grinned. 'But look at it this way, love and stubbornness are better for his teeth.'

Harder on the heart though, she thought as she drove home. But she was grateful to Salty for what he had told her about Colin's childhood. It made it easier to understand him, to feel sympathetic instead of like hitting him with a brick, though she doubted that he would be pleased if he knew that Salty had told her. The same spiky pride and arrogance that had got him through his miserable childhood would just as obstinately want to deny her any knowledge of it. It was the same pride, she realised now, that would never permit him to tell her that he loved her (even on the slight chance that he did) if he thought she was still engaged to Rich. A man as experienced with rejection as Colin wasn't going to open himself up easily for anyone any more. And what surer way of being rejected than declaring your love to a woman already engaged to someone else! He might well tell her that she was 'wasted' on Rich, he might even offer her a 'fling', but beyond that, she was sure now, he would not go.

Not unless she gave him some encouragement. She smiled as she turned into the street where she lived, feeling like she imagined that Salty felt when he picked himself up out of the dirt and started after Gypsy one more time. She couldn't supress a tiny giggle at the thought of what Colin's reaction would be if he knew Salty had compared him to a horse.

Four hours later Anna was grinding her teeth at the realisation that it was impossible to act loving, encouraging, or even stubborn with a person who wasn't even there.

'You don't suppose he had an accident on the highway?' she asked Will for the third time in the hour as she paced circles in the parlour.

'No, I don't suppose he had an accident,' Will said from the easy chair where he was trying to read a weekly news magazine. 'If we got a harness for you and a grinder you could mill all our own flour,' he grinned, and she shot him an irritated glance.

'Very funny.'

'Well, I don't see why you're all steamed up. He's gone shopping. I expect he'll want to take quite a few things along to Guatemala for some of the people we worked with on the dig. Things they can't get easily down there.'

But why should it take six—no, seven—hours?'

Will shrugged. 'Who knows? Besides, he's got Cindy with him.'

'I know.' Anna didn't want to think about that. It was all too easy to imagine what he could be doing for six or seven hours with Cindy Tate—and it didn't entail shopping. She gritted her teeth loudly and Will looked at her, amused.

'Relax,' he advised. 'He'll be home before you know it. If you're worried about him now when he's out on the highway, you're going to be a basket case while he's in Guatemala. Between the guerillas and the army he could end up with a hole in him, like as not.'

'Thank you very much,' Anna snapped. 'I really needed to hear that.' She hadn't given a thought to the political situation. Weren't malaria, snakes, and married women enough without that?

'You really are worried, aren't you?' Will regarded her curiously, all teasing gone.

Anna gave a helpless little shrug. 'I guess I am,' she admitted.

'Fallen for him?'

'Mmmmm.'

Will looked sympathetic. 'Poor you.'

Anna grimaced. 'Thanks for the encouragement.'

Will smiled. 'Would it help if I said, "I told you not to"?'

'Hardly. I've told myself that often enough already, and look where it's got me.' She wandered over to the window again and peered past the curtains. 'Here he is now!'

With the moment at hand she felt a nervousness grip her that she had managed to ignore earlier. What should she do? Blurt out that she was no longer engaged and look hopefully at him waiting for a declaration of his intentions? Suddenly the thought of it seemed preposterous, and her mind groped wildly for something, anything, to say.

The front door banged open and she heard Colin say, 'Go on in the parlour and sit down. I won't be long,' and his feet thudding up the stairs to his bedroom. Anna turned from the window and dropped, anguished, into the chair as Cindy walked into the room.

'Hi, Will. How are things? Hello.' This last was to Anna, but Cindy's gaze slid past her so fast that if she'd blinked Anna wouldn't have thought that Cindy knew she was in the room at all. Damn him what did he have to bring Cindy back for?

'Sit down,' Will invited, nodding at the vacant sofa, and Cindy curled up on it like a rather smug house cat. 'You were gone a long time,' Will went on. And Cindy allowed herself a cat-who-got-the-cream smile and said, 'Colin had *sooooo* many things to do. And he was grateful that I was there to help him.'

'Pity Anna couldn't make it,' Will said, arching her a significant look, but Cindy simpered.

'But of course she wouldn't have been nearly so much help. I know the town so well, and she's a stranger here. She's from California.' She made California sound like the pits, and Anna longed to throw something at her. But the only thing on the table was Will's mother's vase, and she knew she couldn't throw that. It was a pity that there wasn't a book at hand—a great, heavy dictionary perhaps—or that Will wasn't a geologist, the sort who kept rocks on his end tables. She almost giggled at the thought, but immediately sobered up when Cindy delined Will's offer of a cup of coffee and went on to say,

'Colin and I have to leave right away. I'm driving him to Madison to catch the plane, you know.'

'What?' The word was out before she could stop it.

Cindy looked at her almost pityingly. 'It worked out miraculously,' she explained, giving Anna a fixed smile. 'I was going to Madison tonight to pick up Mike at the airport. He was in St Louis at a convention. And since I had to go anyway, Colin asked me to drop him off.'

Miraculous, no, Anna thought, unless God had a very odd sense of humour. But *neat*, yes, it was that. Planned almost, she thought, suspicious.

'You don't mind, do you?' Cindy's voice affected concern, and Anna thought, you're wasted here, dearie. You should try Hollywood. But she managed a carefree smile and said,

'Why should I? Saves me the trip.' She stood up, hoping that she could bolt to the kitchen before she did something to disgrace herself, when Colin thumped back down the stairs and dropped his duffle bag in the entry hall.

'All set,' he announced, and Anna stopped halfway to the kitchen, poised in flight, to stare at him. He wore a pair of tan chinos and a knit rugby shirt, open at the neck, and she found herself tracing the lines and angles of his body, memorising it, remembering it unwillingly from the day she had come upon him shaving, and a tide of red washed across her cheeks before she looked away. Cindy got up quickly and joined him in the entry hall, hanging on his arm and looking up at him adoringly, and Anna thought, I wish Mike could see you now. But she said nothing, stopping with one hand on the doorframe as though she'd been frozen to the spot.

'My regards to Pepe and company,' Will said easily. The only voice of normality in the room, Anna thought, and he levered himself out of the chair and gave Colin a goodbye handshake. 'How long will you be gone?'

'I don't know.' He looked across the room at Anna, his expression closed, and for an instant she remembered Gypsy and thought frantically, What can I do? What can I say? But then Cindy said,

'It's getting late. We'd best be off.'

'Yes.' His eyes were still on Anna but they were bleak and cold. He crossed the room, coming up to her and tipping her chin up, kissing her dispassionately on the lips like a proper fiancé would (emphasis on *proper*, she thought). 'Goodbye,' he said, and Anna shuddered, her mind screaming, 'Don't go. I love you,' her eyes imploring, but her mouth perversely silent. The duty kiss, the cold peck that made more of a mockery of any relationship that they might have had then if he had totally ignored her and had slammed out of the house without saying anything. She wanted to die.

'Goodbye.' Her mouth could scarcely form the words. But he nodded, almost curtly, as though it was all he expected, and turning on his heel, he went out the front door with Cindy, like a faithful puppy, tagging along behind.

Anna didn't move, not even after she heard the car doors slam and the Volvo roar away.

In time, Anna told herself nightly, congratulating herself on getting through another empty day, she would be able to smile and say, 'Colin Davies? Yes, of course I remember him. Nice guy,' or some equally innocuous remark that would prove how little he meant to her. Presently, however, she felt more like a burn victim—raw and vulnerable, all of her feelings exposed.

Will carefully kept Colin's name out of the conversation, keeping her busy with piles of typing and research and asking her questions about how her workshops week at school was coming and whether or not she had her classes prepared and generally being the thoughtful, tactful man she desperately needed at the moment. Jenny, on the other hand, had all the tact of an observant three-year-old. When she found out that Colin had left she plopped down on Anna's bed, looked at her squarely and said,

'See? I told you he was in love with you.'

'What?' By no means of logic could Anna have got from love to Guatemala where Colin was concerned.

Jenny looked at her as though she were dim. 'He

thinks you're engaged to Rich, doesn't he? So what else is he supposed to do? Challenge Rich to a duel? Of course not! So he leaves. Poor Colin!'

Poor Colin indeed! 'It was hardly a case of unrequited love,' Anna snapped. 'Not when he went off with Cindy Tate.'

'Oh bosh Cindy Tate. That was just to make you jealous.'

Anna rolled her eyes. Jenny had read too many romantic novels. To imagine that Colin had run away to Guatemala because she was engaged to Rich when he had always known she was engaged to Rich and had, furthermore, blatantly used her engagement for his own ends while still dallying with Cindy Tate was just too much. Only Jenny could hatch a bitter-sweet plot out of a muddle like that.

'Why didn't you tell him right off that you weren't engaged to Rich anymore?' Jenny demanded, as though Anna were to blame for his trip to Guatemala and not the looting.

Because I couldn't stand the thought of his saying, I told you so, Anna thought. Because falling into his arms like a ripe plum was something I had no intention of doing. Not as long as he believed that commitments were for the birds. 'None of your business,' she told Jenny firmly, wanting out of this discussion before it went any further. 'I've got to wash my hair now. I'll see you in the morning.'

Jenny grimaced. 'Touchy. Touchy. You're taking up where Colin left off.'

Anna stuck her tongue out. 'Scram,' she said, suppressing a grin.

Jenny bounced off the bed. 'I'm going. But I think you ought to write him a letter and tell him you're not engaged. He might take the next plane back. You never know!'

Very funny that. Colin take the next plane back? Ha. More likely it was case of 'out of sight, out of mind.' Exactly what she had experienced when she had come to Belle River and left Rich. It wasn't long before he had become nothing more than a vague memory, a disembodied voice on the telephone. It was probable that she occupied a similar position in Colin's thoughts. If, indeed, she was in them at all. As absorbed as he became in his work—an absorption she had seen at first hand—she doubted that he even remembered she existed. She just wished she could forget him.

God knew she tried. School started and she threw herself into it with as much enthusiasm as she could muster. She was first in the building in the morning, and last out at night. After dinner she closeted herself in her room, making elaborate lesson plans, handouts and bulletin boards.

Will watched her with indulgent concern and finally asked, 'Do they give a prize if your nose is worn off by the grindstone at the end of the first week?' Anna grinned at him weakly, but she didn't stop, just lugged her books upstairs and continued to slog away.

It worked. To an extent. She was so tired by the end of the day that she couldn't stay awake very long and worry about Colin, wonder what he was doing, where he was, how he was. It was all she could manage to curl around her pillow, hugging it because she couldn't hug him, and fall asleep almost at once. She developed a new routine that left her no time to think. She met new people who didn't ask about Colin, and she told herself that she was getting over him, that any day now she'd be able to make an apple pie without expecting him to cut the first piece before it cooled off, without looking for his razor in the medicine cabinet, without hearing Will sing two lines of a current song and expecting Colin to chime in with the words that Will forgot. Well, she told herself three weeks to the day after he left and she remembered him as if he had just left the room, you were wrong.

She never stopped missing him. There was a continual ache deep inside her, so constant that she couldn't remember life without it. It was almost laughable trying to compare this ache with the one she'd felt when she'd left California and Rich. That had been like spraining a finger. This was like losing an arm.

She dragged herself into the kitchen late that Friday afternoon and dumped her books on the table, not wanting to contemplate the long, lonely weekend ahead of her. School days were the best days. Busy work was therapy. Weekends were hell.

'You're home!' Jenny bounced into the room waving something in her hand. 'Ta-da!' she exclaimed and dropped the pale blue airmail letter into Anna's unsuspecting hands.

She would have known the handwriting anywhere. It was as spiky and unique as the man who had written it. Her fingers trembled as she jerked it open.

'What does he say?' Jenny demanded, hopping from one foot to the other. 'Does he say how much he loves you? When's he coming home?'

'Hush.' Anna sank into one of the wooden kitchen chairs and unfolded the letter. It wasn't long, barely a page, and if she'd been expecting, like Jenny was, a declaration of undying love, it wasn't what she got.

'Hot here,' he had written. 'Makes Belle River feel arctic by comparison. We've got bugs like you wouldn't believe.' She could envision him, hot and sticky, shirtless and primitive, and a shaft of longing speared her so severely that it was a moment before she could focus again on the letter in her hand. He hadn't said much more. He went on quite normally about the extent of the looting (not as much as he had feared), and described a design on a potsherd he thought she might like, even including one of his quick, precise sketches that reminded her of sorting his notes when he was ill. He mentioned a great meal that he had had in Guatemala City before he went out to the site, saying he thought she would have liked it, and he signed it, 'As ever, Colin,' which, she thought, was just about as ambiguous as he could get.

'Well?' Jenny asked again, impatience undisguised.

Anna dropped the letter on the table. 'Read it yourself,' she offered hollowly. There was no reason

why Jenny shouldn't. It was about as personal as a
circular from her congressman. Damn him! She jumped
to her feet and, taking back the letter from Jenny who
looked both disappointed and puzzled, she ran up the
steps to her room, tempted to wad it up and throw it
away.

Why on earth had he sent a letter like that? He might
as easily have written it to Jenny herself, or Will or even
Anna's sixth grade class. She sighed and flung herself
down on the bed, kicking off her shoes and rolling over
on to her back, staring at the letter, trying to unlock it,
make it say more than it said.

Slowly this time she read it over from the beginning.
She could hear Colin's voice speaking a kind of
shorthand he sometimes used with her, as though she
could guess the rest of what he meant—a relaxed Colin,
friendly, charming, telling stories as he had done at
Salty's. It was almost as though he was in the room
with her, sitting in the rocker, telling her things that
struck his fancy, sharing his day. She couldn't help
smiling. Then, despite the smile, she felt tears forming,
and she shut her eyes, holding them back, refusing to let
them overflow on to her cheeks in silent acknowledge-
ment of all the days she had spent longing for him to be
there.

He's still not here, she reminded herself fiercely. It's
only a letter. Not a very personal one at that. She
stuffed it carefully into the envelope, putting it in her
top drawer, and shutting it resolutely. She had a maths
assignment to correct, and then some social studies
worksheets to prepare. She had her life and he had his.

But she couldn't help wondering if once Gypsy had
made a slight move toward friendship with Salty—a
benign stare, a slight nudge? But maybe she was just
being fanciful, reading in things that were not really
there.

It was hard not to though when another letter came
the next day. It wasn't any more passionate than the
first, mostly about a rainstorm that had nearly washed
him away, and that he was having to learn how to

weave a hammock which was harder by far than piecing together bits of pots. She could hear him telling the story—hear the wry, self-deprecating humour that would have her giggling, see the twinkle in the dark brown eyes. And she swallowed hard and put that letter into the drawer with the first.

The letters came regularly after that. Nearly every day. Short and chatty, they could have been left lying on the breakfast table, but they weren't. She squirrelled them away in the drawer after rereading each day's again and again. On Saturdays she allowed herself the luxury of rereading them all.

She had got used to his off-handedness. It seemed exactly right now. More right than a 'love letter' or a proposal of marriage or whatever else she might have been hoping for at first. These letters didn't demand anything from her. They calmed rather than cajoled, and if they were meant to seduce and not to lull, she was never sure it wasn't the product of her own mind, even though she hoped it was not. She wanted them to mean that he was trying to trust too, that he was re-establishing the links that had been broken when he left, but she didn't know for sure. Probably she wouldn't until he came back.

She had no idea when that would be. She had asked him once, in her third letter to him. But he never answered, and she wasn't sure about the dependability of mail going to archaeological digs; it was quite possible he had never got the letter at all. So she couldn't say he was ignoring her or avoiding her question.

She had debated for a while about answering them at all. But the temptation was too much for her. So she did—but she tried to match her tone to his. Friendly and non-committal. Cheerful and impersonal. Little Mary Sunshine, that's me, she thought, sending off another one.

But she couldn't squelch the hope that began to rise inside her. If he hadn't wanted to, he needn't have written. He had. She gave the mail box lid an extra flip for good luck. So he hadn't forgotten her. He wanted her friendship, that much was clear. And maybe, just maybe, she thought as she scuffed her way back to the house through the autumn leaves falling around her, he wanted something more. Much more.

CHAPTER NINE

ANNA'S carefully constructed optimism grew slowly but steadily over the next two weeks, built on a series of friendly missives from Colin. The earthquake came on a crystal clear Saturday in early October, a blue-sky-and-golden-leaves day that should have spelled hope rather than disaster. Anna was hanging out the washing, enjoying the snap of the sheets in the wind and thinking that in less than two hours the mail would come and, with it she hoped, a letter from Colin. Funny how a thin blue airmail letter could turn a long, grey weekend into a small Christmas. She pinned the last pillowcase to the line and looked up to see Jenny burst through the gate, ever-present tennis racquet in her hand.

'How are you at tennis?' she demanded.

'Rotten.'

Jenny made a face. 'Well, it can't be helped. I need a partner and you're it. I was supposed to play doubles with Doug in a tournament today only he went to some stupid football game in Madison.'

'I can't do that,' Anna protested, but Jenny was as obstinate as both her male relatives. In ten minutes Anna found herself wearing a pair of terry tennis shorts and a navy knit top that, if it wasn't tournament wear, was at least, according to Jenny, passable. Her playing however, she feared, would not be. During the bike ride over, though, Jenny wasn't swayed.

'It doesn't matter,' Jenny insisted. 'I'll do all the work.'

'Court four,' the official told them when Jenny dragged her towards the courts. 'Five minutes.'

'I can't do this,' Anna hissed, but Jenny had the look of the implacable Fieldings (or Davies), the same one she had seen occasionally on Will and countless times on

Colin, and so she followed her, seeing that all objections were futile.

'Who are we playing, for heaven's sake?' she demanded, catching up with Jenny. 'They'd better not be any good.'

'Cindy isn't,' Jenny assured her. 'I don't know about Mike.'

'Tate?' Anna stopped as though she'd hit a brick wall.

'Of course, Tate,' Jenny said, not looking back. 'Hurry up, will you?'

'You want me to play tennis with Cindy Tate?'

Jenny looked infuriated. 'Not *with* her, idiot. *Against* her. I should think you would enjoy it.'

'Hardly,' Anna muttered. Nothing she ever did with Cindy Tate (or against her) seemed to come out right. And a tennis match was about the least promising thing of all.

'Ah, you're here,' Mike said. 'We thought you might forfeit,' he told Jenny flashing her a grin.

'Never,' Jenny retorted, loosening her racquet from the press. Shades of Colin, Anna thought. Uphold the family honour at all cost, even if it meant dragging in an incompetent to play in the match.

'You're going to be her partner, Annie?' Cindy asked, the blue eyes wide. She looked amused and sceptical, and Anna found herself suddenly *wanting* to win.

'Apparently,' she said coolly, trying for a casual detachment that she didn't feel. Cindy Tate looked exactly as she would have expected—like an advertisement for tennis wear from the pastel pink bow in her hair to the matching pompoms on the heels of her socks.

'Let's get on with it then,' Cindy said, with a smile that didn't reach her eyes. 'And may the best team win.'

Whether it did or not, Anna couldn't have said for certain. Cindy was about as much use to Mike as Anna was to Jenny. It was like playing singles with a human handicap, Anna thought, not relishing her role. She tried to commit as few errors as possible, and was grateful mostly when the match was over. She was as amazed as Jenny when they won.

'I don't believe it,' Jenny said over and over. Anna didn't either. She thought it was mainly because, if her concern had been to be as unobtrusive as possible, Cindy's had been to be as obvious. And every time Cindy managed to stick her racquet up in front of Mike's the ball went too short or too long or too wide, and Jenny managed to pull them through despite Anna's occasional contact with the ball.

'I'll get you in the singles,' Mike told Jenny good-naturedly, wiping the sweat from his forehead and grinning.

'Probably,' Jenny acknowledged, laughing. But Anna could tell that she was pleased, and Anna herself felt on top of the world. It was amazing how you could be a total hindrance, and still feel as though part of the victory was yours, she mused. She bent to tie her shoelace and saw a pair of sparkling white tennis shoes backed by pink pompoms on her eye level.

'Nice game,' she said to Cindy as she straightened up.

'For you,' Cindy said, eyes flashing. 'Be glad you won in this, Annie. You can't win them all.'

Anna laughed. 'I wouldn't expect to. I scarcely knew what I was doing.'

'You didn't know what you were doing when you agreed to marry Colin either, did you?' Cindy demanded.

Anna looked around quickly, hoping to drag Mike or Jenny into a conversation that would eclipse this one, but they were at the far end of the court by the water cooler, and she and Cindy were irrevocably alone. 'I think you already had your chance with Colin,' she said slowly. More than one, it seemed. Maybe it was Cindy who didn't want to share!

'I haven't lost him yet.' Cindy snapped.

Anna stared. 'But—but you've got Mike!'

Cindy smiled demurely. 'True. But Colin was my first love.' She was acting like Anna had stolen him from her, pouting like a child who's had a toy pirated by another youngster.

'I'm sorry,' Anna said coolly, not sorry at all.

Cindy shrugged. 'He'll be my last one, too. I'm pregnant, you know.'

For a fleeting moment Anna didn't make the connection. When she did she felt as though Cindy had slipped a knife in her ribs. 'You are?' It certainly wasn't noticeable.

'Eight weeks.'

Anna didn't say anything. Tremors of understanding rocked her. Colin's baby? Was that what she meant?

'I'm going to love a brown-eyed baby,' Cindy went on relentlessly, her eyes never leaving Anna's face.

Elementary genetics, Anna thought bitterly. Mike had blue eyes; so did Cindy. Guess who had brown? Her teeth came together with a snap.

'I'm sure you understand that this changes things,' Cindy said, her eyes fastened on Rich's ring that Anna still wore. 'When I tell Colin, arrangements will have to be made.'

'You mean Mike might not like a brown-eyed child?' Anna managed a brittle laugh, her earth cracking, shaken to the core.

'Hardly.' Cindy's mouth curved into a plastic smile. 'Think about it, dear. You might want to do something first.' She turned and skipped across the court to the water cooler while Anna sagged on the bench, her world in rubble at her feet.

'Where'd you get to?' Jenny asked when she got home later that afternoon. 'I looked for you after the game and you were gone. Pfft. Just like that.' She snapped her fingers and regarded Anna curiously. 'Were you sick?'

'A headache,' Anna lied. The ache was in her heart. 'Too much exercise for an old lady,' she said, not turning around from the cake she was stirring up. Her eyes were still red from crying, and she knew that if Jenny saw them she wouldn't hesitate to ask.

'I can't believe we really beat them,' Jenny enthused.

'Life is full of surprises,' Anna said. In more ways than one. She was surprised, in fact, how far her hopes had fallen. She hadn't thought she was building them up so high. All on a bunch of letters! A paper universe, and just about as durable. She wiped a surreptitious hand across her eyes, swallowing hard, still scarcely able to picture the rugged, dark haired man she loved (yes, damn it, *still*) as the father of Cindy's child. Another shuddering sigh rocked her. An aftershock.

Jenny absently opened the cookie jar and took out a handful, munching then as she perched on the table. 'Mike did beat me in singles. He's good. Pity he's stuck with Cindy.'

He wouldn't be for long, Anna thought. But she couldn't tell Jenny that. Revelations, when they came, would have to come from the parties involved. And she would have to, like to or not, get uninvolved as soon as possible. Cindy had been right about that. It wouldn't do anyone any good for her to go on pretending to be engaged to Colin when the one person it was supposed to have convinced was now the mother-to-be of his child. She tipped the batter into the cake pans and slapped Jenny's hand away from the cookie jar. 'Save room for dinner,' she admonished, and very nearly dropped the cake pan when Jenny retorted,

'You'd make someone a very good mother!'

'I doubt it,' Anna managed, her stomach twisting. She bolted up the stairs to her room, leaving Jenny, mouth open in astonishment, to shut the oven door.

Anna didn't sleep well that night. The pale blue envelope which came, regardless of Cindy Tate's untimely announcement, for once did not induce any starry eyed dreams of Colin. Instead she lay awake tossing and twisting in the sheets trying to make sense of her life. Her hopes for Colin were as useless ultimately as her hopes for Toby had been, despite all her wishes and all Salty's good advice. It wouldn't have made any difference if she had told him that she wasn't engaged to Rich. By then, even though he might not know it, Cindy's baby (*their* baby!) was a fact. If she had told him things might even be worse, she reminded herself. They might really be engaged, really planning a wedding. How would she feel then?

Not any worse than she felt right now. In her heart she had been engaged to him—as surely as if she had been wearing his ring, not Rich's, on her finger. She looked at it now, its brilliance scarcely diminished in the moonlight, and sighed, slipping it off and setting it on the bedside table.

I would have fought for you, Colin, she thought sadly, if it had just been me and Cindy. Tears welled up in her eyes and she ignored them, letting them course unchecked down her cheeks. But I can't fight a baby and win. I can't fight a baby at all.

'Help,' Jenny said, poking her head in Anna's bedroom door. She looked harassed and grumpy, not at all her usual joyful morning self.

Anna lifted the pillow from off her head, hoping she didn't look as bad as she felt. She hadn't fallen asleep until nearly five in the morning and it couldn't be much past nine yet.

'What?' she asked, sitting up and brushing her hair back from her face. The sun streaming in was waking her up more quickly than she wanted it to.

'I need you.'

'Oh no, not again. One tennis match is enough, thanks.' For life, Anna thought. I never need another one like yesterday.

'Not tennis, dopey. It's Colin's mother. She's downstairs.' She made it sound as though the plague had just entered the neighbourhood.

'Colin's mother?' Anna was stunned.

'You thought we found him under a cabbage leaf?'

'No. But I mean, what's she ... He never said she was ... How'd she happen to turn up? Did she call?' Anna jumped out of bed, nervous but curious. Even knowing that her future with Colin was no longer a possibility, she couldn't quell her interest in Colin's mother. Especially after Salty's description of his relationship with his parents.

'He didn't say. I don't suppose he knew. She never says when she's coming. She just appears.' Jenny was clearly annoyed. 'Anyway, I don't know what to say to her.'

Anna tugged on a pair of white jeans, then noticing the grass stain, she changed them for a pair of brushed denims and a plaid shirt. 'Did you offer her coffee?'

'She's on her fourth cup. Hurry up and come down.'

'Why me?'

'You're his fiancée.'

'You didn't tell her that!'

Jenny face reddened. 'Well, I mean ... Will was gone, and so is Colin, of course, and I didn't know what else to say. Besides she was running him down to me. Telling me he was always going to be dashing all over. So I thought telling her he had a fiancée was a good idea. Don't you think so?' Jenny appeared to be having second thoughts.

Anna made a face. 'Just terrific.' She changed her clothes a third time, this time with the idea in mind that she was supposed to be Colin's intended wife. As such she supposed she ought to try to impress her future mother-in-law. 'So what am I supposed to do now?' she demanded. 'Go down and say, "I'm your son's fiancée. Sorry you've never heard of me"?'

'She has,' Jenny defended herself. 'Now.'

Anna rolled her eyes. She tried to do something moderately sophisticated with her hair, imagining that Colin's mother would expect more than a young woman with long auburn hair cascading down her back untamed. Especially if she had met Colin's earlier fiancée. She was not exactly competition for Cindy Tate. Finally, despairing of anything else, she pulled it back into a french twist and anchored it with a gold barrette. 'I could kill you for this,' she said, fixing Jenny with a malevolent stare, and she was only half joking. Meeting Colin's mother, after what she had heard about her, would be daunting at the best of times. Under present circumstances she felt positively over-whelmed.

She thought her assessment of the situation, sight unseen, was fairly accurate when she finally met the woman. Colin's mother was a tall, fine-featured woman, elegant and tailored. The closest she had ever seen Colin come to his mother's bearing was when he took her to Chicago. She was glad she had tried for a bit of sophistication. It looked like a word that Mrs Davies or whatever her name was would understand.

'I'm Anna Douglas,' she told the older woman who was seated on the couch holding a coffee cup and studying her with equally avid interest.

'Margaret Tanner, my dear. I'm pleased to meet my son's fiancée. I'm glad someone finally told me he had one.' Her voice was decidedly brittle, and Anna thought she couldn't really blame her, finding out that way.

'It was rather a spur of the moment thing,' she excused, sitting down on the other end of the couch. 'We hadn't known each other long.'

'I'm surprised,' Colin's mother said, arching her eyebrows. 'I'd have thought he'd have your background investigated at least. I wonder how he determined you were a paragon so quickly.'

'I—I beg your pardon?' Not knowing Mrs Tanner, it wasn't possible to be certain she was speaking sarcastically. But Anna couldn't see how she could be anything else.

'He wouldn't accept anything less,' Mrs Tanner said, setting her cup down with a thump. 'He didn't accept that other girl he was going to marry—Sassy whatever her name is.'

'Cindy,' Jenny supplied, looking like she could catch flies as she stood propped against the bookcase, listening.

'Yes, Cindy. He wouldn't marry her,' Mrs Tanner went on. 'He said I was the reason. "She's just like you," he told me!' Her voice could cut granite, Anna thought. She thought Colin must have been pretty daring to have told her that. But what did Mrs Tanner mean, he wouldn't accept Cindy? Hadn't *she* jilted *him*? 'He certainly never thought I was perfect,' Mrs Tanner was saying. 'He never forgave a thing. I don't suppose he forgave this Cindy girl a thing either.' She was glaring at Anna now, as though it were all her fault, and Anna, because she thought she should say something, said,

'Well, I don't think . . .'

And Mrs Tanner cut in, 'I hope you know what you're getting into here, my dear. Colin is not an easy person to live with. He's not an easy person to love.' She straightened her slim navy skirt over her knees and went on relentlessly, 'I should know. He was a particularly pesky child.'

Anna heard Jenny gulp clear across the room. 'He was, Mrs Tanner?' she said, remembering her own thoughts based on Salty's recollections. She had seen him as lonely. His mother had remembered him as a pest.

'He certainly was. Whoever would have thought that such a clingy, sickly little boy would grow up into *that*?'

What Mrs Tanner meant by 'that', Anna wasn't quite certain, although the journey from being 'clingy and sickly' to becoming the hard, rugged, handsome man she knew must have been a long one. 'I didn't know he was ill as a child,' she said softly. The morning light played through the leaded glass windows, casting a softening light on Mrs Tanner's hard features, and for an instant Anna saw a reflection of Colin in them.

'Good heavens, yes. Sore throats, croup, tonsillitis, chicken pox, measles. You name it, Colin had it.' She sounded disgusted even today. 'It was the first of my unforgivable traits, I'm afraid,' she laughed somewhat bitterly. 'I didn't fancy myself a nurse, so generally I had the help take care of him. He's never failed to remind me how I failed him as a mother. So when I talked to Gareth when I was with Howard in New York last week and he said Colin had been ill, I thought it was my "motherly duty" to make it up to him. And now he's not even here!' She made it sound as though Colin had got well just to spite her, and Anna thought she could understand why Colin was reticent when it came to mentioning his mother. And if he thought that Cindy was like her——?

'Who's Gareth?' she asked.

'Colin's father. We were divorced yeàrs ago. I've been married three times since. Another of my unforgivable traits.' Mrs Tanner sniffed. 'Colin is absolutely rigid about the sanctity of marriage. I hope you'll enjoy being married to him. Imagine being married to a veritable saint!'

Or a flaming hypocrite, Anna thought. If he believed so strongly in marriage vows, what was he doing with Cindy Tate? 'You mean he didn't approve of your divorce, Mrs Tanner?' she asked cautiously, wanting to understand correctly.

'He doesn't approve of me, period,' Mrs Tanner said, aggrieved, and catching the momentary hurt look on his mother's face Anna thought that, despite her brittle tones and harsh laughs, Colin's rejection had indeed hurt her. 'You're right. Our divorce really set him against us both. But especially against me because, well, frankly, I left Gareth for another man. Gareth was a bit dull really, for all he had an exciting sounding job.' She sighed, as if the memories were none too pleasant. 'Do you mind if I smoke?'

'Get Mrs Tanner an ashtray, please, Jenny,' Anna said. Jenny grimaced, as though she were being asked to miss the best episode of her favourite soap opera but, at Anna's glare, she went.

With nervous hands, Colin's mother lit a cigarette and drew a deep breath. 'I don't know why I'm telling you this,' she said, exhaling slowly. 'I suppose because you look so innocent.'

So much for the sophistication, Anna thought wryly. But Mrs Tanner went on, 'You'd better hope you are innocent, dear, or Colin will make your life miserable.'

What was she supposed to say to that? Anna wondered. I'm innocent? She smiled a bit worriedly at Mrs Tanner who took another puff of her cigarette and shook her head. 'I mean it in the way of a warning, I suppose. He expects a great deal of the people he loves.'

Anna watched specks of dust floating in the sunlight, swirling madly, with about as much direction as her thoughts. She wished Mrs Tanner would go. She needed to think. The Colin she had been hearing about this morning did not seem to be the sort of man who would have fathered Cindy's child. Was it possible that he had not?

'I don't suppose I'll ever really understand him,' Mrs Tanner shrugged her elegant shoulders. 'I hope you will, my dear.' She didn't sound as though she thought it was very likely, but she got to her feet and stubbed out her cigarette and offered Anna her hand. 'I'm glad to have met you, Miss Douglas.'

'I'm glad, too, Mrs Tanner,' Anna said sincerely. 'I hope I'll understand him, too. I think, perhaps, I'm beginning to.'

'I hope so. I hope I haven't made things worse by telling you all this,' his mother said. 'I seem to have done very little right where Colin is concerned. Probably telling you all this was a mistake too.'

Anna didn't think so. She walked Mrs Tanner to the door, promising to write Colin and tell him that his mother had come to 'nurse' him, privately thinking that Mrs Tanner's revelation that she had to be back in Madison before lunch to meet her husband diminished a great deal her contention that she was prepared to stay and care for Colin. But what did it matter, really. It was enough, Anna thought, that she had come. She had certainly provided Anna with plenty to think about.

Mrs Tanner gave her a dry peck on the cheek. 'I'm delighted to have had this chance to talk to you. I wish you luck with my son. You'll need it.' She got in the car and rolled down the window saying, just before she drove away, 'Don't rush to make me a grandmother. I feel old enough already.'

An hour ago Anna would have been able to say quite confidently that the damage had already been done. A grandchild was on the way. Now she wasn't so sure. She watched the rental car disappear around the corner and walked back to the house and up the steps. Jenny was leaning frozen against the bookcase, and Anna reached out and gently closed her mouth.

'Don't look so stunned,' she chided, though she was feeling a bit dazed herself.

'Wow!' Jenny breathed. 'I can't believe that woman is related to Colin.'

'Don't tell me you're going to subscribe to the cabbage leaf theory yourself?' Anna grinned, privately thinking that while his mother might not look much like him or act at all like him, she went a long way towards explaining why he was the way he was.

'It's a thought,' Jenny said, laughing. 'Imagine just dropping in because your husband happened to be at a medical convention in Madison. Now she'll go back to Atlanta and we won't hear from her for another two years or so. What a mother!' She shoved herself away from the bookcase and said, 'I think I'll go hit a bucket of tennis balls. Want to come? It always helps to clear my head.'

Anna declined. 'No, thanks. I think tennis muddles my thinking rather than clears it.' Or yesterday's had anyway. One thing was certainly true: her head needed clearing and her conclusions re-examining. She had some very strong doubts now that Cindy Tate's baby was Colin's at all. Not if he felt the way his mother claimed he did about the importance of fidelity in marriage. After all, she realised, though she had seen him with Cindy in an incriminating embrace, she had only Cindy's word for what was going on, just as she had only Cindy's word about the baby.

Hadn't Colin got 'engaged' to her in the first place to put off Cindy Tate? In fact, if one discounted Cindy's testimony, it was possible to see Colin's dealings with her in a new light completely. Jenny had said that he must be jealous of Rich and that he was probably trying to make Anna feel jealous too by hanging around with Cindy. Could that be the truth? Anna gave a little skip around the room. She remembered him muttering, 'The hell with Cindy Tate,' words she couldn't imagine him uttering if he were really still in love with her. Maybe it was true.

But if it was, what was she to do about it? He was miles away—thousands of miles—it wasn't as if she could cross the hall to his room and say, 'I think you've misunderstood . . .' Or could she?

Well, not the same way exactly. But she could write him a letter. A wholly different one than the jolly impersonal sort that she had been sending in response to his. Did she dare?

She stopped at her desk, staring at the stationery sitting on top of it, wondering if she had the courage. She could be all wrong. She could write him and say, 'I think I should have mentioned that I'm not engaged to Rich anymore, but I was afraid to,' and it could blow up like a land mine in her face. He could say, 'I told you so,' and completely ignore the vibrations that she had sensed so strongly between them, or he could take her admission to mean that she was ready for an affair whenever he got back. He could make her life an even greater hell than it was now, she thought grimly. Or he could make it heaven.

Which do you want? she asked herself. Or do you have the guts to even give him the option? Safety first, Rich would have cautioned her. But, she thought wryly, she hadn't learned his lesson very well. She sat down hastily at the desk and took out a piece of paper.

'Dear Colin,' she began, 'I have something important to tell you . . .' and she told him—all of it—how she'd broken off her engagement in Chicago, how she'd been afraid to tell him before, how she was afraid to tell him now but she had to, even if it meant that he didn't really want to be bothered with her again and, with a daring almost as great as the emotions that had prompted the letter in the first place, she signed it, 'Love, Anna.'

She sealed it and took it to the post office before she could indulge in second thoughts. And as she walked slowly home she felt like someone who has slipped on a loose stone at the top of a mountain. She was tumbling in a headlong fall, unsure whether open arms or disaster awaited her at the bottom.

The only thing to do, she told herself firmly over the next few days, was to put it entirely out of her mind. And if she didn't succeed, it wasn't for want of other things to think about or because she didn't try. On the contrary, she spent hours working out a science experiment kit for her students, did more typing for Will, and helped Jenny plan an extravagant birthday party for William to be held on Friday night.

It was this last activity which took up most of her time. Jenny liked elaborate plans and would have ended up by inviting half the town if Anna hadn't put the brakes on her flamboyant enthusiasm. But even Anna couldn't keep Jenny from inviting practically all the University faculty and staff—including, of course, the Tates.

'Why not just the Anthropology and Archaeology Department,' Anna had suggested. They were clipping along through the supermarket with Jenny throwing paper plates, napkins, and other various luxury items in their trolley and dollar signs were flashing in Anna's head, but Jenny just shook her head and protested,

'But then the Hugginses and the Powells would be hurt. And I couldn't have a party for Will and not invite the Staffords and . . .' the list went on and on, as did the growing pile of items in the grocery cart. Anna closed her eyes in dismay and slammed directly into Cindy Tate.

'You're coming, aren't you?' Jenny demanded as they were sorting themselves out.

'Of course,' Cindy said, giving her one of the famous blinding smiles that Anna had grown to hate. 'I wouldn't miss it. How've you been, Annie? Jenny?'

'Busy,' Jenny said, flipping a carton of sour cream into the cart. Anna nodded in agreement, hoping that they could move on without any further conversation, but when Jenny said, 'What's next on the list?' and Anna pulled it out of her pocket to consult it, Cindy said,

'No ring?' and looked at her with wide, innocent eyes.

'What?'

'I was wondering what you'd done with your ring, Annie.' She looked like a lion ready to pounce, and Anna didn't mind lying at all.

'Just getting it cleaned,' she said blithely. She hadn't put it back on since the night she'd thought that Cindy was having Colin's baby, and she wasn't going to now. If she wore a ring again, it would be Colin's own, not Rich's. And if Colin never offered her a ring, there wouldn't ever be one, but that was her business and Colin's, not Cindy's. But she didn't imagine for a minute that the other girl was fooled.

'Cleaned, hmmm?' Cindy asked with just the right amount of scepticism, and Anna said,

'Yes. Please excuse us. If this is going to be the party of the century, we'd better get on with the shopping.' She nudged an open-mouthed Jenny on up the aisle, leaving Cindy Tate to think what she would.

'Speaking of people I wish you hadn't invited,' she said to Jenny as soon as they were out of Cindy's earshot.

'Too late now,' Jenny said. 'Sorry about that.'

Not any sorrier than I am, Anna thought, as the week wore on. She would happily have avoided Cindy for the rest of her life, and knowing that she was going to have to spend all of Friday evening in the same house with her, being pleasant, cast a pall over the entire week. That coupled with the knowledge that probably by Friday, at the earliest, Colin would receive her letter, made her edgier than a sailor about to walk the plank.

She kept thinking, I wonder if he got my letter today? Does he care? Was I wrong to send it? She wished she could put it out of her mind and concentrate on the party, but that only brought her round to remembering that Cindy was going to be there, and that made her blood pressure rise another few degrees. She wasn't fool enough to think that Cindy would let the evening go by without saying something that would upset her. She hadn't missed an occasion yet. If only Anna felt more confident of Colin she wouldn't let it bother her. But confidence was one thing she lacked. She had written him the letter on the slimmest of hopes, the barest glimmerings of trust. But more than that she didn't possess.

It wasn't possible though, once the party began, to wonder if Colin was sitting in a jungle somewhere reading her letter when she was busy taking coats, making small talk, pouring wine, and running back and forth to the kitchen to replenish the trays of goodies.

By ten-thirty she thought she might make it through the evening without having to talk to Cindy Tate at all. She had seen the Tates come in around nine and had promptly ducked into the kitchen on the pretext of opening another bottle of wine, and since then she had managed to keep to whatever room they were not in, putting as much distance as possible between Colin's ex-fiancée and herself.

It wasn't possible to avoid conversations about her though. She was cutting pieces of birthday cake and passing them out when the wife of one of the sociology professors remarked, 'I hear the Tates are going to have a baby,' to another woman who nodded and said, 'Let's hope it helps their marriage. Something better, from what I hear.' Anna felt her stomach muscles clench, and her hand shook as she sliced through another piece of the cake.

Was the Tates' marriage really on the rocks? It was possible, she supposed. Mike would have had to be blind not to see Cindy's play for Colin. And maybe he'd heard the Cindy-spread rumour that it wasn't even his baby. Anna felt nauseated. For the first time since she had talked to Colin's mother she wondered if she could have been wrong. Maybe Cindy had been telling her the truth after all.

She thrust the cake knife into Will's hand and, ignoring his look of concern, she bolted for the kitchen saying, 'Excuse me, I'll be right back.'

Hanging on to the sink she took great gulps of air, reeling at the sudden thought that if the Tates divorced, Colin might marry Cindy after all. Calm down, she told herself. But a shudder ran through her, and she closed her eyes. The door to the kitchen opened and Cindy Tate walked into the room.

'Jenny told me I'd find more crisps in here,' she said, waving an empty bowl. Anna nodded dumbly pointing to the cupboard next to the refrigerator. Cindy bent to get a bag out, then straightened up and dumped it into the bowl. 'Colin called last night,' she said conversationally, her ice chip blue eyes glittering. 'I told him about the baby.' She crumpled the empty bag with the same ease that she was crumpling Anna's world. 'I notice you still aren't wearing your ring. Smart girl.' And with a brittle smile she gave Anna a regal nod and marched out of the room. The door swung hollowly behind her.

CHAPTER TEN

IT wasn't only nuclear attacks that could cause total devastation, Anna discovered. Little verbal bombshells like the one Cindy Tate had just dropped did the job just as well. Her fingers curved tightly around the back of the kitchen chair, her whole being rocked as she considered the implications of Cindy's parting shots.

The least of it, she decided, was that when Colin got her letter he would have a good laugh about what a naïve little idiot she was. Perhaps, she thought grimly, he was even chortling now. There was the chance that he had got it today after all. More to the point, she realised, the truly devastating thing was imagining him married to Cindy Tate. If rumours were correct and she and Mike were having problems, and if Colin was truly the father of her child (and, Anna conceded wryly, that could cause problems in a marriage) there was every chance that Cindy would be the new Mrs Colin Davies. Regardless of what his mother thought. It wasn't exactly comforting, but maybe he had learned how to forgive after all!

It hurt too much to try and laugh about it—far worse than Toby's betrayal had. That had been like a toothache—this was mindblowing. The only greater pain she could imagine would be to be there and see it happen. A wedding between Cindy and Colin! She shuddered at the thought. She would have to leave before he came home. Find an apartment. Move away. Quit. Anything so long as she didn't have to watch Colin marry Cindy. And she would have to do it soon, because if he knew about the baby, he wouldn't wait long. How long until Cindy could get a divorce, she wondered. How unutterably stupid she had been, thinking that his letters meant something. If he'd wanted to he could have 'phoned. He 'phoned Cindy Tate.

'Have we got any more rosé?' Will asked, poking his head in the door. 'Say, are you all right?'

'Fine,' Anna lied, brushing a shaky hand through her hair. 'I'll look. I think there's another bottle or two in the pantry.'

'Good. Bring 'em out if you find any.' Will's head disappeared after he gave her a quick grin and a probing look, one which said that he suspected that all was not well but he'd have to wait until later to check for sure.

Grateful for something to do, Anna rummaged through the pantry, finding a bottle of rosé and a two-litre bottle of white rhine. She shoved open the swinging door and edged her way past several laughing and talking bodies to the buffet in the dining room where Will was dispensing the drinks.

'Here you are,' she shouted above the din. 'It's all I could find, so I brought some white too.'

Will turned from pouring a glass for one of the English professors and said, 'Thanks. The more the ... Good God! Look who's here!'

Anna's head swivelled towards the entry hall wondering who would be dropping in to celebrate at nearly midnight. The bottle of wine slipped unnoticed from her hands.

'Colin!' She couldn't have said it aloud, only breathed it, like a person swallowing a dagger. Her face was a mirror of stark agony. Was he here for Cindy already? That fast? Only last night had she talked to him, and tonight he had come. Come for the mother of his child. She wanted the floor to open beneath her. Frantically she glanced around for Cindy. She was standing near the fireplace with Mike and two other men, talking and laughing until she looked up and saw the tall, lean man hovering in the doorway, duffle bag in hand. Then she turned white.

Colin hadn't seen her yet. His eyes were roving over the crowd, doubtless searching for her. Anna wondered what he would do when he found her. Surely he couldn't carry her away immediately. Not with her husband standing only a few inches away. She wrenched her gaze from Colin to look back at Cindy, expecting to see the white face change to triumph once Cindy had recovered from the shock of seeing him. Instead she saw a stunned and greyish face rivalled, she imagined, only by her own. Confused, Anna looked back at Colin to see what he would do.

Colin wasn't even looking at Cindy Tate. He had dropped the duffle bag on the carpet and was wending his way through the crowd coming towards her! 'All this way just for my birthday?' Will asked, grinning and flinging an arm around his cousin's shoulder. 'Have a glass of wine. Rosé, I think. Anna seems to have smashed the white.'

Anna stood, mesmerised, oblivious to the people mopping up around her, eyes fastened on the man before her, hardly believing he was real. Her hands wanted to reach out and touch him, feel the hard sinewy muscles, the stubbled cheeks, the unruly hair, but they didn't, hanging instead like lead weights at her sides. He was browner, leaner, hungrier looking than when he had left. His eyes, dark and with a feverish glitter, bored relentlessly into hers.

'Hmmm?' He didn't seem to know what Will was saying. He shook his head as though to clear it and reached for Anna's hand which went unresisting into his. 'No ring?' he rasped.

'No.' It was scarcely more than a whisper. She doubted he could have heard it above the raucous laughter and clinking glasses, but he let out a long breath, as though he had been holding it for some time.

'No Rich?' he persisted.

'No.'

He turned then, dragging her after him towards the door. 'Come on. We have to talk.'

'But . . .'

'No buts.' He ploughed through the throng like an icebreaker, and Anna threw a helpless glance back at Will who shrugged and grinned, and a curious one at Cindy Tate who seemed to have traded her whitish grey complexion for a vaguely green one, before she was hauled into the entry way.

'Get a jacket,' he commanded, tugging on Will's.

'Where are we going? You can't just come in here and haul me off like some sort of caveman. What are you doing here? Haven't you got the wrong girl?' She was babbling, spluttering, competely befuddled, and he jerked another coat off one of the hangers and began stuffing her arms in it.

'It's not mine,' she protested.

'We're not stealing, just borrowing.' He continued tugging it on her and began to do up the zipper as though she were a three year old child, and coming to her senses momentarily she flung his hands away.

'I can do it myself.'

'Fine. Do it and come on.' He put his hand against her back and steered her out the door before she could catch a breath.

The brisk chill and spitting snow of early November weren't nearly the shock to her system that Colin was. The jolt of moving from a warm, noisy house to a heavily clouded, frosty night was nothing compared to the jolt she felt whenever he touched her. He steered her out to her VW and motioned her to drive, jack-knifing himself into the passenger seat beside her. The electricity flowing between them was so intense that she couldn't even remember how to start the car. Colin took the key and started it for her.

'Can you handle it now?' he asked with a mocking indulgence that maddened her. How was she supposed to remember mundane things like how to drive her car when he turned up out of the blue, ignored the woman who was apparently the mother of his child, and practically kidnapped her from under the noses of everyone on the entire faculty?

'I can handle it,' she said, valiantly trying to pull her mind together. 'Where to?'

'Salty's.'

'He's not there,' she protested. 'He couldn't even come to Will's party. He went to see his sister in Minneapolis for the weekend.'

'So much the better,' Colin grated. 'Let's go.'

'But . . .'

'Just drive.'

It was useless to argue. She took in the grim set of his hard mouth, the harsh, almost angry planes of his face which were shadowed in the dim glow of the street light, and shrugged, put the car in gear and backed out of the driveway.

'Would you mind explaining . . .'

'Later,' he bit out. 'Just get us there safely. If I tried to talk about it now, I might wring your neck.'

'What?' She turned to stare at him, convinced that he'd lost his mind. If anyone did any neck wringing tonight, it wasn't going to be Colin.

Colin didn't answer. He kept his eyes resolutely on the road, as though the white line was the only thing that interested him. Getting no response, Anna stepped down harder on the accelerator, determined that she would get them there as soon as possible and find out what all this was about. What did he want to know about the ring for anyway? Surely he couldn't have got the letter this afternoon and have flown up here tonight. That was existentially impossible however wonderful it might be.

'Not so fast. You'll kill us both,' he muttered finally. 'What do you know about driving in snow anyway?'

'Not a thing,' Anna said blithely. 'I've never done it before.'

Colin groaned. 'Pull over. I'll drive.'

Anna ignored him, turning on to the gravel of Salty's road, gripping the steering wheel for dear life.

'I said, *pull over*!'

'Make me.'

It was the wrong thing to say. So quickly that she had no way of stopping him, he reached over and yanked the key from the ignition. The car sputtered and died, sliding across the snow-covered gravel with Anna ineffectually jamming her foot on the brake.

'Into the skid!' Colin yelled. 'Turn into the skid!' He grabbed the wheel, jerking it from her hands. 'Stop braking so hard!'

Frantic, Anna braked harder. The car skidded across the shoulder, bounced down a small incline and stopped. With the aid of a tree.

'My car!' she wailed. 'Look what you did to my car!'

'I did? *I* did?' His bellow was full of the most righteous indignation. '*I* told you to pull over.'

'You pulled the key out!'

'Only when you wouldn't,' he argued. 'It's your fault.'

'You come home from Guatemala, drag me out the door like some kidnapper, wreck my car and then have the nerve to blame it on me!' She couldn't stop the hysteria from bubbling in her voice, and she wrenched the car door open and plunged out, scrambling up the bank.

'Where the hell are you going?' Colin scrambled out his side, took a quick glance at a badly smashed bumper and fender, and took off up the hill after her.

Anna was totally unequipped for hiking through the Wisconsin winter countryside. The open-toed sandals and floor-length navy velvet skirt that she had donned for Will's party tripped her up before she even reached the road. She stumbled through the icy slush, cutting her toes on rocks and scratching her legs on the bare brush. When Colin swept her up into his arms her anger almost dissolved in relief.

She could feel the heavy thud of his heart through both their coats and the warmth of his breath on her face. With everything in her being she wanted to press her face into his neck, let herself luxuriate in the feel of him, in his nearness, his warmth. But she couldn't. Not with everything still unsettled between them. She drew back and gasped,

'Put me down.'

'No.' He was striding along the road now, carrying her as though she weighed no more than a sack of feathers. She had no recourse but to wrap her arms more tightly around his neck and pray that her best intentions wouldn't have melted by the time he set her down. They hadn't more than a quarter mile to go before they reached Salty's. But it seemed like a hundred to Anna before he swung her lightly down on the front porch and said, 'For God's sake, stay put. I'll crawl in through the back window.'

He disappeared around the side of the house, and Anna shifted from one foot to the other, wriggling her toes in the fluffy whiteness, feeling the melting iciness beneath her feet and thinking, he needn't have worried. In these shoes she wasn't going ten feet. Not that she wouldn't have liked to.

A light flicked on and the front door swung open. 'Come on in,' Colin said, reaching out to give her a hand so she wouldn't slip on the wet snow. The warmth of Salty's living room enveloped them both and Anna thought how unfair it seemed. It would be even harder to resist him here, to pretend that she didn't care.

He had turned away from her, as though he wanted to put off the inevitable as much as she did, and was busy making a fire in the fireplace. She took advantage of the situation to let her eyes feast on him. Probably, she reminded herself, for the last time. She had done some figuring while he was carrying her, and what she had figured was that while he was most likely going to marry Cindy, he couldn't just walk into Will's party and pirate her away from her husband. And he probably felt some compunction about explaining to Anna what he intended to do. Explaining best done in private—hence, his arrival, her virtual kidnapping, and their presence in Salty's living room. And the ring? Probably he was annoyed that she hadn't bothered to tell him before. It seemed plausible anyway. Neat. Tidy. If only she didn't ache so just from looking at him.

She kicked off her shoes and padded into the kitchen trying to wring the wet hem of her skirt out into the sink. It seemed wiser, too, to get out of the same room as Colin. That way she felt less temptation to go up behind him and run her hands over the curve of his spine, to knead the muscles of his shoulders, to touch the dark hair curling against the back of his neck.

'Here,' he said into her ear, making her jump a foot.

'Put these on.' He shoved a pair of jeans, a belt, and a navy crew neck sweater into her arms. Her mind went back immediately to the last time he had lent her his clothes at Salty's, when he had fastened the belt around her waist himself. Her face burned at the recollection and, judging from the way Colin was looking at her, she thought he was remembering too.

'I'll be in the living room,' he said abruptly, deaparting before she could utter her thanks.

She took her time changing, leaving the high necked, silky white blouse on under the sweater, its lacy collar softening the effect of the jeans and sweater. She cinched the belt tightly and rolled up the cuffs, prolonging her return to the living room as much as possible. There was something about it that reminded her of entering the lion's den, something distinctly unnerving, and she stood for minutes with her hand on the door knob before she mustered the courage to enter.

He was standing with his back to her, hands clasped behind him, staring into the fire. Classic pose before the delivery of bad news, Anna thought. How to tell her tactfully that it had been nice to know her but there was the little matter of Cindy and his baby and . . .

'How long?' he demanded without turning around.

'How long what?'

'How long haven't you been wearing Rich's ring?'

The ring again. What difference did that make? 'What do you mean?'

He spun around. 'I mean,' he said slowly as though he were speaking to a halfwit, 'How long since you told ol' Rich to shove off! How long since you came to your senses?'

'What do you care?' She flared, knowing a momentary relief that he definitely had not got her letter. At least he wouldn't know what a fool she had been. The relief was quickly overshadowed by her anger that he seemed to want to focus the conversation on her. It was Colin who owed the explanations—not the other way around!

'I care because I love you, damn it!' Colin shouted,

hands on hips, eyes glittering with the look of a man not in love, but war.

'What?' Anna felt her world spin. 'But . . .'

'And I decided that if you'd finally given up on that stupid notion that you ought to marry Rich Howell,' he went on relentlessly, 'that there was finally a point in coming back from Guatemala!'

'*That's* why you came?'

'Of course.'

'Then you *did* get my letter?' She shook her head, confused. 'But I don't see how you could have if . . .'

'What letter?'

'I wrote you a letter. I said in it that I had broken the engagement with Rich when we were in Chicago and . . .'

'Chicago!' It was a howl of rage.

'I was going to tell you,' she defended herself.

'Why didn't you?' He was pacing the floor, exactly like the lion she had been fearing, and she edged towards the kitchen door.

'Because you always behave like such a beast,' she shouted at him. 'And you would have said, "I told you so".'

Colin grinned wolfishly. 'Probably,' he admitted ungraciously. 'But my God, woman, the hell you've put me through just so you wouldn't have to hear it!' He glowered at her and she moved a little closer to the kitchen. Then, without warning, his hands dropped to his sides, and the look changed, softened. 'Chicago, huh?' he mused, as though toying with the ramifications of that idea. He smiled. 'Come here,' he coaxed, moving away from the fire and sinking down on to the couch.

Anna looked at him sceptically.

'Come on. I won't bite. I promise.' She heard the words, but it was his eyes which truly beckoned, urging her away from the door. For a long moment she couldn't move. Neither her legs nor her mind would entirely accept what her ears had heard. Had he said he loved her? Slowly she shook her head, and Colin held out a hand, saying, 'I do, you know, love you. Trust me.' It was hesitant. A plea. But it was enough.

Bewitched, Anna moved across the room as though she were being tugged by an invisible thread. Colin took her hand and pulled her down beside him so that they were barely touching, resting his arm along the back of the couch behind her shoulders. 'That's better,' he murmured, his eyes tracing the line of her lips until she thought she would go mad with wanting him to kiss her. His mouth crooked slightly, as though he knew her thoughts, and he shook his head.

'How did you know, then?' she asked. 'About Rich and me?' She was trying to be rational, to sort things out when really all she wanted to do was snuggle closer and feel the hard warmth of his arms around her. But she sensed his tightly controlled restraint and knew that he was wise. First they had to talk. So she contented herself with touching him with her eyes, believing finally that the time would come when she could do it with her hands.

'Cindy told me,' he said.

'Cindy?'

'I called Mike last night because some of the housing arrangements for the college students fell through,' he explained. 'He wasn't in, so I gave the message to Cindy. And just as I was about to hang up, she said in her best feline voice, "By the way, I see you couldn't hang on to Annie either." ' He grinned, his arm tightening around her. 'At first I couldn't figure out what she meant. Then she said, "She isn't wearing your ring anymore, you know." I could hardly wait until morning to catch the next plane back here. I didn't know for certain, but I thought that maybe—just maybe—you'd broken it off with Rich.'

Anna's brow furrowed as she remembered something. 'But what about the baby?'

'What baby?'

'She didn't tell you about the baby?'

Colin looked mystified.

Anna rubbed her nose, suddenly unwilling to go on. She could hardly say, 'Your baby.' Especially now.

'She's going to have a baby, you know,' she began cautiously.

'So what?'

'So,' Anna paused, hearing the fire crackle, wondering if she dared, then blurted, 'She said it was yours.'

'*She what?*' Colin looked stunned, then furious.

'Well, she implied it anyway. She talked about wanting brown-eyed babies when she and Mike are blue-eyed and . . .' Anna's voice trailed off leaving her feeling like a first-rate idiot. Colin looked like he might explode.

'How the hell could you even think a thing like that?' he demanded, and there was nothing in his voice now to remind her that only moments before he had said that he loved her and that she should trust him.

'Because you were kissing her and she said we'd have to share you, and then you took her to Dubuque with you, and she always seemed to be around hanging on you, and, damn it all, what would you think?' Anna shouted back, jumping up and going to stand with her back to the fire, hugging herself tightly. The fire snapped and crackled, but she was in more danger of getting burned on the couch just then as far as she could see.

'I was kissing her? Colin looked baffled. 'What on earth are you talking about? Cindy Tate holds about as much appeal for me as a snake does.'

'That's what I thought. Once. But when I went to get a drink in the English Building the day we went to *Othello*, I saw you two on the steps. And you weren't shaking hands!'

'Oh Lord,' Colin muttered, burying his face in his hands, then looking up ruefully at her. 'You saw that disgusting little piece of flirting?'

'Flirting? She looked like she was going to climb inside your shirt!'

'She damn near did. I thought I was getting a drink and she thought we were taking up where we left off three years ago.'

'It was all her idea?'

'Of course it was.' But he had the grace to look embarrassed. 'It's not my fault if she throws herself on me and swears that this time it will be different, is it?'

'She said that?'

'Yes.' He grimaced, as though he would rather not talk about Cindy at all. But Anna wasn't dropping it there. Cindy Tate needed discussing. There were too many other instances that she'd had her hand in to just leave it there.

'And, of course, you turned her down?' she said sceptically.

'Naturally. I was besotted with you. What do you expect me to do? Make love to a woman I can hardly stomach being around when all I can think about day in and day out is how to get you to break off your fool engagement to this veritable saint on earth?'

'You weren't in love with me then,' Anna protested.

'The hell I wasn't!'

Anna thought the jungle sun had definitely affected his brain. His grip on reality seemed to have slipped. 'You thought it was convenient to pretend we were engaged,' she reminded him. 'That's all.'

He smiled audaciously. 'It's not all,' he assured her. 'But it was convenient—a way to get behind enemy lines, so to speak.'

'What?'

'I didn't really intend it to happen,' he explained, still smiling. 'But I'd been trying to figure out how to convince you that you'd be better off without Rich, and I just happened along at the right time. It was inspired really.' He looked so pleased with himself that she longed to throw a shoe at him, and regretted having left her sandals in the other room.

'You said it was to put off Cindy Tate.'

'It was supposed to do that too,' he conceded. 'But apparently without success. Just exactly what has she been saying to you?'

Anna wondered if she could remember it all. 'She saw

me standing there after she was kissing you, and she said you two had something going. And,' she shrugged, 'it seemed to follow that you must have. I mean, you were going over there all the time, and driving her places, and having lunch with her.'

'Mostly they were meetings with Mike about the field work seminar,' Colin said. 'And then, I didn't want her to think I gave a damn about her anymore, so whenever she asked me for a lift or sat down at my table in the Union, I just went along with it. Dumb me.' He shook his head ruefully. 'Anything else?'

'You took her to Dubuque with you the day you left. You said that some people would miss you! And she took you to the airport!'

'I was furious with you,' Colin said. 'I thought you'd go into Chicago, see Mr Wonderful, tell him it was all off, come home and fall into my arms. Instead you waved that damned ring in my face all evening!'

'I did not!'

'You didn't take it off!'

'I was afraid to.'

'Why?' All the ferocity of seconds ago vanished. Instead she heard a gentleness that astonished her. He got up and came to stand beside her, putting his hands on her shoulders, looking deeply into her still troubled eyes. 'Why?' he repeated.

'Because of Toby.'

'Who?'

She tugged him down on the hearth rug, sitting with her legs outstretched and he turned sideways to lay his head in her lap. 'The man in my past,' she explained.

'I thought Rich. You mean there were more?' He grinned.

'Before Rich. The reason for Rich.' She had never talked to anybody about what Toby had meant to her. Not even Rich. But she needed to tell Colin now. 'Toby wanted a fling but he didn't want marriage.'

'And you did.' It wasn't a question.

'Yes. Until I heard about his other woman, the baby he refused to acknowledge was his. Then I only wanted out. But he thought it was a lark. Good times and no strings. All that.' She recalled how she had felt when she realised that all her hopes and dreams were not shared by Toby nor ever had been. 'He soured me on handsome men,' she said, brushing her fingers lightly through Colin's hair. 'He was definitely the original Mr No-Commitments.'

'Like me.' Colin's voice was soft, but matter-of-fact, and Anna looked down at him, seeing the harsh lines of his face now softened by the firelight and something more, and nodded.

'You scared me to death,' she told him.

'Me?' He looked astonished. 'Why? The way I yelled at you?'

'No. The way you made me feel.'

'Tell me.' He was smiling now.

'I didn't want to feel that way. All sort of shivery and aware. I wanted to miss Rich, and the moment I saw you I thought I'd been hit by a truck.'

'That bad?' Colin grinned. He nestled his head more closely under her breasts and traced erotic circles on the palm of her hand.

'Terrible. Truly. I thought absence would make the heart grow fonder with Rich. But once you appeared, I couldn't even remember what he looked like.'

'Good.'

'Good? It was awful.'

'Thank you very much,' he said drily. 'I could say the same thing about you.'

'Nonsense. You wanted nothing to do with me.'

'Because you scared me too.'

He hadn't looked scared, but she didn't contradict him this time, and he went on, 'I was attracted to you from the first. I liked the way you stood up to me, snapping back. But, you're right, I didn't want you there. I didn't want any woman complicating my life, much less one I found attractive. All the women I'd ever cared about weren't worth it—

Cindy, my mother—so I certainly didn't need you.'

'You made that quite clear.'

He laughed shortly. 'But when you insisted on staying, I was in no shape to fight you, and I thought, why not? I might as well take advantage of it—have a fling.' He looked a bit sheepish.

'Was that why you kissed me that night?'

'Yeah. I told myself it was to prove that a fling with you would be fine, and not any different than a fling with any other woman. I figured you were engaged but, so what? Cindy'd been engaged to me but that didn't stop her sleeping with whomever she wanted.' He closed his eyes and she saw pain in his face.

'I'm not Cindy,' she said quietly.

'No. I could've guessed that. But I didn't want to. At first I even wanted you to be like her, to justify my actions, so to speak. But then you pulled back and ran away and, my God, you were gone for hours!' He looked up at her, anguished, remembering. 'I was terrified that something had happened to you, I worried myself sick. And believe me, I had plenty of time to realise that you weren't another Cindy. That's why I said I was sorry—for treating you that way.' He turned his head to stare into the flames. 'That's when something more than a fling first began to sound good to me.'

'Will said you didn't want to be tied down,' she told him.

'Will talks too much.'

'Well, he was only telling me what I could see with my own eyes,' Anna retorted, defending him. 'One minute you were making a pass at me and the next you acted like you didn't know I was alive. What was I supposed to think other than that you were just fooling around?'

'I knew you were alive,' Colin said drily. 'You were in my every damned waking thought.'

'How pleasant for you,' she said sarcastically. 'It sounds like you enjoyed it.'

'I didn't enjoy it a bit. It was torture. I was falling

in love with you and I sure as hell didn't want to. Also, you were engaged to Rich, who had, as far as I could tell, none of the faults known to man, and every time I pushed my own suit, you clung to him a bit harder.'

'I didn't know what you wanted. I thought all you were interested in was convincing me that I didn't love Rich so I would have an affair with you.'

'That is what I wanted. Once. But I damned sure didn't after a while. But you were holding me off all the time.' He grimaced. 'I thought I understood what makes women tick, but you sure confused me. One minute I would be kissing you and I'd be sure you were responding to me, and the next you were cutting me dead. I thought I was losing my mind. But when you went to Chicago, I really thought you'd call it quits with Rich and I'd at least have a chance.' He glowered up at her. 'But the ring stayed firmly in place and you acted like you could hardly wait 'till Christmas so you could see him again and jump in bed with him!'

'I never!'

'Make allowances for jealous rage, can't you? I wasn't thinking too clearly at that point. You see, I'd got it all figured out how I was going to propose to you that night, after you'd broken off with Rich, and then you didn't!'

'I didn't trust you yet,' Anna said. 'I'd been brainwashed quite well by Cindy Tate. She knew exactly how to play off my insecurities. I kept comparing you to Toby, and it was all too easy to doubt you meant any more by your kisses than he did.' She stroked a hand through his hair, brushing it back off his forehead. 'What was she doing it for anyway? I mean, if she wasn't really in love with you?'

Colin shrugged. 'I broke our engagement. I suppose she thought this was a nice way of getting even.'

'You broke it? I thought she had.'

His mouth twisted. 'She had as far as I was concerned when I caught her sleeping around. But I was the one to make it official. She seemed to think it was okay to "share" ... I didn't.' He sighed and shook his head. 'I guess I can see why you didn't trust me if you thought what she told you was true. But all I could think was that you really didn't give a damn. That's why I left. What was there to stay around for?'

Anna smiled. Jenny had been right after all. How pleased she would be to know it! 'I'm sorry,' she told him.

'But you said you wrote a letter.' He looked perplexed. 'If Cindy had you convinced I was a skunk, what made you change you mind?'

'Your mother.'

He sat bolt upright. *'My mother?'*

'She dropped in one day last week. To nurse you through your malaria, she said. Jenny told her I was your fiancée and I spent part of the morning talking to her. She said I'd have to be a paragon to keep you.'

Colin stared. 'She said *what?*'

'Oh, she told me that she'd been unfaithful to your father and that that, among other things, had destroyed your relationship with her. And then she said that you hadn't approved of Cindy Tate for the same reason. She seemed to think you expected sainthood for any woman you planned to marry, and she warned me accordingly. Later, when I got to thinking about it,' she told him, smiling, 'I didn't see how, if you felt that way, you could justify having a relationship with a married woman. So I started rethinking everything Cindy Tate had said.'

Colin grinned. 'Good for Mother. She owed me one. I shall have to thank her for it. It's the only good thing she's ever done for me, convincing you!'

'I think she regrets the way things are between you,' Anna told him.

'She ought to. She never gave a damn about me my whole life—only when it suited her. When I was seven she dumped me at the hospital to have my tonsils out and never reappeared. My dad picked me up three days later.' His expression was hard, cold, and Anna ached for the rejection she knew he had felt. She remembered, too, his reactions to being in the hospital in the summer. 'Don't go,' he had muttered. 'Stay with me.' Thank God she had.

He laughed suddenly.

'What's funny?'

'I was just thinking how we owe our current understanding to Cindy and to my mother! I hope they both appreciate how useful they've been.'

'Your mother will, anyway,' Anna said. What Cindy did or didn't do wasn't important. There was no conceivable way she could hurt them now.

Colin reached out and drew her against him between his knees so that his chest curved around her back and his hands slid up under the sweater and blouse she wore, caressing the silky softness of her skin. 'We'll have to invite them to the wedding,' he murmured, his breath teasing the tendrils of hair curling around her ear.

'What wedding?'

He drew back suddenly and twisted her around to face him. 'What do you mean, what wedding? Ours.'

'I think you forgot something,' she grinned.

'Such as?'

'Proposing.'

He shook his head. 'Nope. You had your chance for that the night we came back from Chicago. You blew it. If you want any proposing done around here tonight, you'll have to do it.' He was smirking, teasing her, but Anna saw suddenly that it made a great deal of sense.

'You're right,' she said. 'The reason I got engaged to Rich was that I couldn't think of any reason not to. So if I actually ask you to marry me, then I must have a reason. To marry you, I mean.' She was considering this thoughtfully, and Colin groaned, rolling his eyes.

'I'm sorry I mentioned it,' he muttered. 'I'll ask. I'll ask.'

'No.' Anna held up her hand, shushing him. 'I will. Colin Davies, I love you. Will you marry me?'

'God, yes, woman,' he bit out. 'Why were you so slow?' and he crushed her in his arms.

She tried to say, 'I only wanted to be sure,' but she'd hadn't the strength or the inclination to get the words out.

They rolled back on the rug, arms and legs entangled, stroking, caressing, loving each other, until Colin dragged himself away to murmur, 'God, how I've missed you. I thought I'd die in Guatemala without you. Loneliness is hell on earth.'

She kissed the line of his jaw. 'I missed you too. The letters were wonderful, but they weren't enough. I was so lonely without you.'

'Me too.'

'You won't be,' she told him. 'Not ever again. I promise.'

In the flicker of the firelight her watch said four a.m. Anna rolled tighter in the blanket, punching down the lumps in Salty's rather incredibly lumpy couch. Colin was asleep in Salty's bedroom, having collapsed there while Anna was taking a hot bath. The toll of his long trip had affected him more than he wanted to admit. They had talked for another hour, whispering the things they had longed to say to each other and had never dared to before. But finally Colin's eyes had begun to droop and his yawns grew larger and soon Anna heard less words and more gentle snores.

'Go on to sleep,' she had told him. 'It's what you need.'

'What I need is you,' Colin had protested, but hadn't argued further when she had shoved him down on to Salty's narrow bed except to say, 'What if I wake up and you're gone?' It was meant to sound light, teasing, but Anna heard the anxiety in it. How could she not, knowing what he had gone through growing up?

She shook her head. 'No,' she said very firmly. 'I'll always be here. Too late now. You're stuck with me.'

He had smiled and closed his eyes, and Anna had gone off to run her bath, too keyed up to even contemplate sleep.

And now she heard a rustling noise which woke her very pleasant dreams. Rolling over she saw Colin, wrapped in a blanket and nothing else, shuffling across the room towards her.

'You are,' he murmured almost to himself. 'Here, I mean.'

'Always. What's wrong?'

'I need to know something.'

'What?' He looked so serious that it scared her. What obstacle to their happiness could he have thought of now?

'Do you keep promises?'

'Of course.' Didn't he trust her even yet?

'I seem to remember your promising me something.'

As far as she could remember she had promised him her life forever more. What else did he want?

'You said I wouldn't be lonely any more,' he said softly. 'And I was.'

'Just now?' She couldn't help smiling, and reached up a hand to draw him down on the edge of the couch.

'Yes.'

She moved over until the couch buttons poked her in the back, and Colin silently slid his lean, hard body alongside her.

'Still lonely?'

'Sort of.'

She giggled and tugged the blanket out, rewrapping it around both of them. His arms came around her, holding her close, their bodies touching from cheek to toe. 'Now? she mumbled into his hair, delicious feelings of love and longing coursing through her body.

'Better,' he conceded. He shifted, then groaned. 'It's lumpy,' he complained. His lips teased hers, moving to kiss her chin, her jaw, her ear, then coming back unerringly to her mouth again.

She shrugged, snuggling beside him, loving the warm,

hard feel of him against her, convinced at last that this man was the right man. 'Loneliness or lumps,' she offered, tickling his ribs.

He grinned and bit her ear. 'Lumps,' he growled.

It was the last sensible thing either of them said for quite some time.

You're invited to accept 4 books and a surprise gift Free!

Acceptance Card

Mail to: **Harlequin Reader Service®**

In the U.S.
2504 West Southern Ave.
Tempe, AZ 85282

In Canada
P.O. Box 2800, Postal Station A
5170 Yonge Street
Willowdale, Ontario M2N 6J3

YES! Please send me 4 free Harlequin Romance® novels and my free surprise gift. Then send me 6 brand new novels every month as they come off the presses. Bill me at the low price of $1.65 each ($1.75 in Canada)—an 11% saving off the retail price. There are no shipping, handling or other hidden costs. There is no minimum number of books I must purchase. I can always return a shipment and cancel at any time. Even if I never buy another book from Harlequin, the 4 free novels and the surprise gift are mine to keep forever.

116 BPR-BPGE

Name _____ (PLEASE PRINT) _____

Address _____ Apt. No. _____

City _____ State/Prov. _____ Zip/Postal Code _____

This offer is limited to one order per household and not valid to present subscribers. Price is subject to change.

ACR-SUB-1

Experience the warmth of...

Harlequin
Romance

The original romance novels.
Best-sellers for more than 30 years.

Delightful and intriguing love stories
by the world's foremost writers
of romance fiction.

Be whisked away to dazzling
international capitals...
or quaint European villages.
Experience the joys of falling in love...
for the first time, the best time!

Harlequin Romance

A uniquely absorbing journey
into a world of superb romance reading.

No one touches the heart of a woman
quite like Harlequin!

You're invited to accept 4 books and a surprise gift Free!

Acceptance Card

Mail to: **Harlequin Reader Service®**

In the U.S.
2504 West Southern Ave.
Tempe, AZ 85282

In Canada
P.O. Box 2800, Postal Station A
5170 Yonge Street
Willowdale, Ontario M2N 6J3

YES! Please send me 4 free Harlequin Presents® novels and my free surprise gift. Then send me 8 brand new novels every month as they come off the presses. Bill me at the low price of $1.75 each ($1.95 in Canada)—an 11% saving off the retail price. There are no shipping, handling or other hidden costs. There is no minimum number of books I must purchase. I can always return a shipment and cancel at any time. Even if I never buy another book from Harlequin, the 4 free novels and the surprise gift are mine to keep forever.

108 BPP-BPGE

_____
Name   (PLEASE PRINT)

_____
Address   Apt. No.

_____
City   State/Prov.   Zip/Postal Code

This offer is limited to one order per household and not valid to present subscribers. Price is subject to change.   ACP-SUB-1

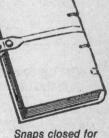